madness

Fiction Novel

Madness

Abdenal Carvalho

Copyright 2020 © Abdenal Carvalho

Title: Madness

Author review

Author cover

Category: Fiction Romance / 107 Pages

This is a work of fiction. Its purpose is to entertain people. Names, characters, places and events described are products of the author's imagination. Any resemblance to real names, dates and events are coincidental.

This work follows the rules of the New Spelling of the Portuguese Language. All rights reserved.

The storage and / or reproduction of any part of this work is prohibited, by any means - tangible or intangible - without written consent by the author. Copyright infringement is a crime established by law No. 9,610 / 98 and punished by article 184 of the Brazilian penal code

SUMMARY

Chapter 1 - Abandonment 7

Chapter 2 - See-O-Weight 27

Chapter 3 - Memories 35

Chapter 4 - Meeting 51

Chapter 5 -- The Interview 61

Chapter 6 - The Trial 75

The End 99

End 104

∞∞∞ 104

Chapter 1 - Abandonment

His wanderings through the streets of the metropolis of Pará, sometimes under heavy rain in a hot and humid climate, at other times under the scorching sunlight that burned his aging skin, darkened by the dense temperature that mercilessly punished him during that miserable pilgrimage. It was a burden of despair and many bitter memories of the past.

As well as a filthy bag over his shoulders, full of various junk found in the garbage scattered throughout the path he used to pass. He gathered everything that seemed useful, according to his crazy ideas, feeding on the remains of food found in the bins located in front of the beautiful houses, where he would certainly never enter.

He recognized that he had no value as a person, he was a penitent already resigned to the poverty in which he had lived for a long time. That night, like so many others, he decides to sleep in one of the several existing squares, to give his tired body a rest on the cardboard he carried inside the dirty burlap bag in which he kept his few belongings, he was not the only one to wander around those sides , the streets were full of beggars.

Therefore, it was necessary to share space with others, sometimes even using brute force to intimidate the most dangerous and separate a small space for yourself to find rest. The government created popular restaurants that sold a meal for less than two reais, a very affordable amount for those who had nothing. At noon, there was a long line of hungry people to buy a dish made, paying with coins received from alms.

They were given to them by those who passed through the narrow streets of the city center, there gathered dozens of beggars who also wanted to quench the hunger that ate at them inside. Despite this, more than a plate of food was still needed to help him and the others who lived inhumanly, thrown out into the open like sewer rats, unclean and unhygienic, due to the abandonment in which they found themselves. What these poor devils really needed from the authorities was a policy plan that would allow them to have good quality shelter, food and medical care and that would be guaranteed permanently.

Not just momentarily. Whenever he satiated his hunger, he went in search of new alms, it was a daily routine, he spent the whole day from side to side with his hands outstretched to anyone, begging for help. His resting place was the well-known square called Republic, located close to the shopping center, between the avenues President Vargas and Assis de Vasconcelos, surrounded by several skyscrapers and vast vegetation, most of which are tall mango trees.

At that time full of ripe fruits that served as food for people like him, forgotten by society. There, dozens of poor people spent most of their time together or individually, consuming alcoholic beverages. Chatting away or simply in confused daydreams of a confused mind.

Numb by the effect of alcohol. Sunday was a good time to collect many coins. Several people walked around the place and sympathized. It was really a sad situation in which the bastards lived and helped them as they could. The cold winter afternoon prevented the sun from appearing and the heat did not dare bother. But the cold was persistent in making him shiver and wanting to keep warm at all costs.

What was impossible for someone in complete abandonment. That he didn't even have new and clean clothes to use, sitting in a corner watching the swaying of the trees around him. He saw the world go round between sips of strong drink, remembering the beginning, how it all started. Luís Gustavo was the eldest son of a riverside family.

Coming from low Amazon, one of the many islands on the banks of the Amazon River and his childhood as the seventh son of an illiterate fisherman who only knew how to cast his fishing nets over the water to collect schools of fish and feed the family, he was miserable.

Fishing was the father's routine. While the boys harvested açaí from the many existing palm trees around the island, they who, like him, grew up like wild animals and adapted to wildlife. They knew nothing about modernity, the cultural poverty in which they lived was extreme. It was true that he was not hungry, but the food was watered the same things every day, there once lost, they saw something beyond the usual fish with wild fruits, and chicken.

When he turned ten, he ran away from home, hitchhiking on a fishing boat, arriving in the capital. Where he spent all his adolescence. He worked at Ver-O-Peso, the largest and most important free fair in Latin America.

Madness - Fiction Romance

Mandatory stop for large vessels and easy access to the inhabitants tourism. A place where a fearless boy worked hard to survive amid all kinds of dangers. Including criminals, drug addicts and traffickers. In that place he was lucky to meet Naomi. A wealthy businesswoman who used to visit the place once a month. Accompanied by your private driver and two security guards, to buy fruits, vegetables and fish.

She learned to admire that little boy who was always very helpful and met his needs with diligence. She felt sorry to see him in that sad situation, living practically in the open. Sleeping on the empty stalls of the market. When they retired in the late afternoon. Every time I went there I saw him dressed in the same weather-worn shorts.

Wearing a Hawaiian-type sandal, whose heels were already corroded by too much wear and a red T-shirt. Stained and with some tears in sight. With immense compassion she proposes to the boy that he move in with her, which he gratefully accepts the opportunity. He had studied at the island's little school, while living in low Amazon, he learned to read and write.

But only the basics, nothing that qualified him to start his studies in the capital without a selective exam.

However, everything started to work out. With Naomi's support and knowledge he was engaged at all costs in the fifth grade of the first grade. From where he could progress in studies until he reached college, which was actually his biggest dream. In the room she received from her adoptive mother there were all kinds of toys, she took care of her appearance. He gave her new clothes and shoes and everything a boy her age needed to be happy.

As she had no children in the two previous marriages, she was a very wealthy widow and wanted to find an heir. He should keep all his assets, take over his properties and continue his empire, and he saw this possibility in him.

The poor boy, who was born on the banks of the Amazon River and had the audacity to flee to a distant place and lived for a long time among strangers, finally had the chance of his dreams before him. To win in life and become an important man, luck smiled at him and opened his arms to him. It came to him in the form of many opportunities and he would certainly use it.

Well, at least that's what I had in mind. Despite so many ways to have fun as any teenager would do, he spent most of his time locked in his room. Studying for the exams of the private school in which he was enrolled. It was indeed very dedicated.

At the end of each year, the result was always positive, his approval was always guaranteed, to the pride of the one who bet everything on him. Upon completing eighteen he completed his complementary studies and faced the entrance exam. He registered as a candidate for a vacancy in the most important medical, law and engineering schools in the City.

He did not want to take a preparatory course, he felt prepared to face the exams, and so he did, to his surprise he was approved. It passed first in all higher education institutions. In the three chosen areas, and it went to his head in such a way that he was unable to bear it. Instead of celebrating the immense achievement, he would lock himself in the room and from outside you could hear his screams. He was maddened, exclaiming the same sentence he spoke as soon as he saw the result.

Madness - Fiction Romance

Euphoric phrases for his approval. Madness was the prize for such a victory. Even with the many efforts to try to remedy the sad situation, nothing could be done to change the mental imbalance that occurred over the young man, he who tried so hard to properly take advantage of the opportunity that fate decided to give him.

He could have reached the peak of his luck. Shine like a shooting star, get on the podium and lift the cup like a winner. But he was prevented from experiencing the greatest moment of his life.

It seemed that he was really cursed to be nothing important, destined to be a nobody, a failure. He was the son of a riverside fisherman who was born and raised by throwing his net in the waters of the Amazon River, resigned to his poverty, with misery hovering around that old rotten shack.

And partly consumed over time. In part, by termites and moths, without being bothered by their uselessness as a human being. He was the type that contributes nothing to human evolution.

Now he has become as useless as his father, completely mad. He was admitted to the most renowned hospitals for treating the mentally ill in the State, under the supervision of the most renowned specialists in the field, however, all efforts to cure him were in vain.

— We are sorry, but nothing can be done to at least remedy this situation.

The brain membrane has been disrupted and neurons are unable to function properly, causing paralysis in much of the brain. Unfortunately the patient's condition is irreversible

— But is there really nothing that can be done to try to change this terrible state of health, of my son, doctor?

— I am sorry to tell you that here in our country, there is nothing that can be done

Naomi felt a deep love for Luís, as if in fact she was his biological mother and she would not give up on him that easily. Following the guidance of the medical team, he left with him to the United States in search of a miracle, but he did nothing. When they returned, she ordered all the mansion's employees to keep the boy's real health in full secrecy, and so it was done. Luís, in his early youth, had an irreversible disorder that led him to live in complete darkness. Trapped in deep mental confusion.

His intelligence succumbed to the darkness that blinded his whole understanding. He completely lost track of reality. He started to live in an unreal world, stopped in time, the moment he read his name at the top of the list of those who passed the best and most popular courses. All at major universities in the region. His neurons could not withstand the electrical discharge of the strong emotion he felt.

And his brain seemed to have reached its maximum charge. Something broke inside his head he spent all the time seeing or hearing confused voices and figures. He spoke to himself and gestured as if someone really was his listener, the large covered space located in the center of the square had been built more than a century ago to beautify that place, but decades later. It ended up serving only as a refuge for the shirtless who did not have a roof to rest from their daily labors.

After begging for bread outside. And that was where he lived, his home, his home, because he lived like a mangy dog, repudiated by everyone around him. The whole situation was pitiful. But he, like all the others who lived in a similar way, did not even realize the deplorable state h Or in the beautiful garden that completed the mansion's luxurious decor.

It was located on Avenue Braz de Aguiar, a noble neighborhood in the city. Always accompanied by a nurse exclusively to assist you in any emergency, as well as for your exclusive company. The professional took his shift with another daily. All attempts to keep the patient in a clinic specializing in the treatment of mental illness have been exhausted without success. Since the patient did not show any improvement and, in most cases, he fled the site without anyone noticing. This, which led Naomi to decide to keep him on a tight leash at home and accompanied twenty-four hours by people specialized in that type of service.

Several years have passed since that tragedy occurred in the socialite's life. She dreamed of having an heir to leave all her assets. Coming from an important part of society, people from extreme social levels, former men and women of unparalleled economic power.

He bet on that dying man all his hopes, now unsuccessful. Naomi Luana Guimarães Velasco, was heir to two of the most important families in Pará. From the times when all economic power in the Northern Region of Brazil revolved around the rubber cycle. Their ancestors were owners of large sums of land where rubber trees were cultivated. Trees from which the latex is extracted, in the form of a very pasty milk, and from it the so coveted rubbers were used to supply the growing Brazilian market, as well as other international markets.

Becoming the biggest exporter of that product, immensely enriching the well-known "rubber lords", a title given to the great owners of rubber plantations. His wealth and prestige was widely known both in Pará society and throughout the country, where he owned several companies. Through which he moved millions of reais and multiplied his assets even more. However, despite all this power, it could not be prevented that such disgrace would destroy his home. Reaching the one he adopted as his future successor. She was a woman of many possessions and aptitude for business.

But with no luck in love and in everything related to the heart. Still in his youth he lived a stormy passion that was scorned by the family. And she suffered bitterly the pain of separation under the threat of being disinherited and losing, because of that, the right of succession in her parents' vast empire. e was in.

He lay on cardboard, staring at nature directly in front of him and seeing old memories in the form of images that no one else could see. Because they were only his, they were engraved on his troubled mind and for him they were all real. And he continued to watch them, passing like a movie. The psychiatric hospital's dark room was his resting place after leaving the place of martyrdom.

The narrow room, filled with torture equipment, was feared by most patients with severe mental disorders. They, who, even though they were mad, clearly knew how terrible the pain of the electric shocks they received from nurses by doctors' ordinance, as treatment for what they called demonic manifestations.

Naomi, who, before giving up on him, interned him there in the hope of curing him, almost goes crazy when she sees him in that situation. Not all the money in the world seemed to be able to cure him of that damn disease.

At that moment, she realized how much material goods sometimes do nothing. And in that particular case, he felt powerless. Because none of his resources are sufficient to save his son. That madness. For she loved him immensely, even though he was not a seed of her guts. In the months that followed, he just vegetated, spent all the time he was awake sitting in some corner of the house.

After being forced into pain to give up the great love of her life, she devoted herself completely to studies and then to the administration of inherited goods. Locking yourself in a world where love was forbidden or something disgusting. Her second great love was epic and it happened after she met that poor boy. A survivor who even came from humble origins struggled to stay away from all the perversity that existed on the streets of the big city.

Especially living close to people with bad character. That ranged from pickpockets to the cruelest criminals, addicts and drug dealers who circulated daily at the Ver-O-Peso free market. The postcard from Belem do Pará. She loved him as a son from the first meeting. Admiring your commitment to serve spontaneously and always with a broad smile to customers.

The same ones that usually thronged in front of the fruit and vegetable stalls there. He helped traders to serve their products to interested visitors to the fair in exchange for food and some change. Everyone admired him for watching him struggle daily to survive honestly. And not committing serious crimes as was often the case for other minor offenders.

That because they did not want to fight, they assaulted and even physically attacked many who passed by, even with the frequent action of the police, this practice was constant.

When you asked him to come to your house. Then he asked her to accept being his son, the happiness he felt when he heard a yes in response was immense. He thought to himself that he would finally have secured his succession, since he had not married. It was the last Guimarães Velasco, after that the lineage would come to an end.

Luís has since become the long-awaited heir to the traditional Velasco family and his legacy would be to continue the legacy. To the important name of that generation of great entrepreneurs.

And everything would have gone as planned if he had not succumbed to profound madness, however it happened and nothing could be done to the contrary, not even all the resources used were able to bring him to his senses. Who knew that young man who looked healthy, had an enviable physique.

Assisted by the best doctors in the most expensive health plans he would come to present such a mental weakness. To the point of not supporting the emotion of an unexpected achievement like that.

During the time that several treatments were done, nothing brought the desired answer. The necessary result for the purpose of reverting the sad state he was in. Many resources were spent without any improvement in his clinic. They gradually made the adoptive mother lose hope of seeing him restored from mental faculties again. Luís was admitted to a specialized clinic in New York City, in the United States, where Naomi had many contacts and had been a client for many years. Staying for a long time, returning from there without any significant improvement. This failure largely diminished Naomi's hope for a possible recovery.

With that, he decided to give up the sick person and set out on a new attempt to find an heir to continue the legacy he received from his parents. After all, despite her more than fifty years of age, she still had an enviable physical and mental health. There would still be plenty of time for that purpose. As a measure to get rid of the current problem, the poor devil was finally admitted to the public hospital Julian Moreira.

Reference in psychiatric treatment. However, in a violent way, based on electric shocks and terrifying psychological pressures. The businesswoman's insensitive decision was due to the fact that she did not want to be criticized by those who criticized her.

They commented on the type of adopted child, they denied it. They did not think it was ideal to serve as heir to all their immense wealth. In the opinion of the rest of society.

The ideal would have been to give that opportunity to one of the many orphaned children in the various orphanages scattered throughout the city. And not to a kid found on the streets. She educated him correctly, preparing him to leave nothing to be desired when it comes to taking over business. His main goal was to prove to the critics that his choice would have been the right one and that everyone was wrong. Seeing the protégé's sudden madness ruin all his plans was terrible. Furthermore, there is a risk of demoralization in the face of those who eagerly awaited to laugh at their imminent failure. All of this made his pride and duty to defend the good name of the Velasco speak louder. Taking her to take drastic measures to get around the situation.

So she chose to remove him from the scene, inventing a huge lie for his disappearance and locked him up in a madhouse. Without the protection of the wealthy businesswoman and left to the care of strangers who cared little for her good.

Luís started to be treated in a violent way as were all the other lunatics. However, that same year of state elections a new government was installed. And many changes have been made in various sectors of public administration. And in the area of health it was no different. The first measure to be taken by the new ruler in order to guarantee the economy was to authorize the closure of the hospital.

Where dozens of mental patients were kept in private prison. Dismissing a vast number of civil servants.

Throwing into the streets the disoriented who, because they do not have family members with financial or psychological conditions to deal with such individuals. They remained wandering aimlessly through the streets and avenues of the city. It has become common to see them scattered everywhere.

On the sidewalks and gutters, alleys and corners, like abandoned dogs and with no one to worry about the damn fate that awaited them each new morning. With the changes that have also occurred in the state penitentiary system, from which countless detainees have been released. Violence in the city has increased considerably.

And with that, the routine habit of changed radically. Thus, people like Naomi who belonged to the elite of society stopped exposing themselves.

They stayed away from places considered dangerous, and that included the old Ver-O-Peso fair. Where Luís spent part of his adolescence and luck smiled at him, leading him to be richly graced with the opportunity to be adopted and achieved a huge achievement, the same one that for not supporting melted his brain. Therefore, it became impossible for the two to meet.

Since she circled the city in her luxury cars, while he wandered around like a poor devil, with his filthy bag over his shoulders, full of the garbage collected wherever he went. Instead of the old linen clothes, he wore filthy rags.

The odor was unbearable for the nostrils of those who approached him, instead of the expensive perfumes he simply had the rot of the damp teeth moistened in the sweat of his body without any hygiene. In its filthy appearance, the true face of misery could be clearly seen.

As well as all the poverty that followed him closely, nothing remained of the beauty he possessed as a young man and lived in wealth. With the perks that luck chose to help you. Until, due to bad luck or the irony of fate, he was deprived of the right to continue enjoying such stewardship. The madness that came suddenly over that unfortunate one came at the very moment when he intended to give his protector a reason to be satisfied. Happy to have adopted you. This would be his glory day, which he would never forget.

But, contrary to his expectations, he ended up forgetting everything. Who he really was and what he did throughout his existence until the moment he lost his mind. Thrown out by Naomi and then by government officials who had no intention of continuing to spend public money on unbalanced people like him, he lived in the open.

Abdenal Carvalho

He was more of a dying man taking up space in the vast square of the square, where several times he traveled alongside the one who welcomed him. When I was still a child full of so many dreams and hope. It was the end of the afternoon, the heavy rain passed and only the drops of water that leaped from above the green grass in front of him remained. Falling over the trees and sliding through their leaves, accompanied by a cold wind that boldly bothered him, even though he was lying down.

At that time, on the filthy floor of one of the many other centenary bandstands existing in that place, the republic square was very old and dated to the beginning of the twentieth century. There were many monuments that were scattered throughout its length were beautiful. They dated from the times of Portuguese visitation in the region. Its history bears the mark of several battles and fights. All against those who tried in vain to conquer those lands. Before he was finally taken by the madness that ended all his dreams.

The poor devil who was now begging along the paths of the beautiful city of mango trees had been an excellent scholar. And he knew the origins of his people like no other.

He loved Pará, his homeland, the exuberance of its vast vegetation, rivers and typical foods that nothing could compare. The people of Pará can be seen as true warriors, overcoming countless adversities.

Managing to survive countless lists and reach the present times successfully. Having fallen in love with his roots, he had already prepared a work to be published shortly after his graduation from the three colleges he intended to attend.

He wanted to acquire academic degrees and practice professions, but he would have literature as a hobby, where he would write his novels and short stories, highlighting where he was born. One more objective went down the drain, as it would never achieve this goal.

His brilliant mind would be consumed by madness and would be lost in the vast dark of empty thoughts. His neurons were disconnected to the point that he was no longer so sublime. Lying in complete discomfort on filthy cardboard. With his gaze fixed on the infinite he could contemplate, blurred images were almost totally undefined.

Lost between reality and the darkness of madness that hung over his confused mind. Very numb by alcohol, with distorted ideas, coming from a very distant past. The memories came and went suddenly. They were lost in the shadows of an obscure mentality, attached to the unreal.

To a world of fantasies and details that his disturbed imagination created and prevented him from perceiving the terrible situation in which he found himself.. He was a walking dunghill, what little was left of what was once, certainly could not bear to face at least a little of the real that surrounded him in an imperceptible way.

His beard and gray hair hardened by the large amount of accumulated dirt, due to the few baths taken. Good hygiene was rare during his penances during the days spent under neglect. Since the doors of the psychiatric hospital closed. The afternoon finally says goodbye. And in its place comes the night with its mysteries. And like a lost soul he moved from side to side.

With uncertain location, under intense serene that appeared after the downpour that fell hours ago. Flooding the lower parts of the poor neighborhoods and creating mud puddles on the deserted streets of people of good nature. The night darkness facilitated the action of the bandits and there were many assaults there.

The victims were almost always people unaware of the danger of circulating at an inappropriate time in a square full of idlers.

Looking to get some change to support the damn addiction to which they were slaves. From teenagers to adults, everyone was addicted to drugs. Police action has become insufficient to even intimidate them. The less it represses crime that just increased, the more and more. He saw everything and thought of doing nothing to defend anyone, even under the effects of the madness that prevented him from reasoning correctly, he was smart. He understood that in order to live on the streets without being harassed by criminals, it was necessary to adapt to the law of silence. If you pass for blind, dumb and deaf.

The night is gone and a new morning begins in the same routine as always. His walking slow. Carrying the old burlap sack over his shoulder, he seemed to carry all the weight of the world upon him. The promenade on the long square was full of dry leaves and fruit. All very mature, falling from the trees with the strong wind blowing during the dawn.

With the ripe mangoes he could eat, it was his breakfast provided by God, free and juicy. The artisans had already arrived at the site. They prepared their stalls to sell their craftwork. They were necklaces, bracelets, rings, clay vases and many other trinkets that they created.

They sold to passers-by who spent mainly on weekends and holidays. Periods when many events took place in that place to distract the population, usually idle with news. A large stage was being built to soon receive singers and artists from the land who would perform.

And they would do their free shows as a form of entertainment for the public, all free. While none of it started and after satiating his morning hunger, he withdrew from there and headed towards the streets of commerce in an attempt to beg the alms that would later circulate.

Doing your usual weekend shopping. A short time later I was already sharing space with dozens of other beggars. Running out of coins on the busy street João Alfredo, on the corner of Santo Antônio. Where street vendors and visitors flocked among the crowded stalls and shops.

Full of consumers because of the promotions and low prices they had, their preference was to settle in the same place and place on the floor, right in front of them. A bowl so that those who passed would sympathize and throw some change in it, as they believed that it should not disturb and it worked very well. At noon, sometimes under almost unbearable heat, at other times under threat of rain.

He usually gave up begging and went back to his old place of refuge, Republic square. And that Saturday was no different, he returned at the same time and in a hurry. Because I still wanted to beg among the participants who would be there. Watching the singers, making their presentations.

Dozens of people watched and applauded the show, while he and several others asked for any form of help. Everything was valid, even the smallest value of the offered currency was acceptable, nothing was rejected.

However, among the crowd of spectators were the thieves covered with evil intentions. With the intention of stealing the belongings of the unseen and, usually, the final balance was always quite pompous. At five in the afternoon, under heavy rain, the onlookers dispersed. The festivity ended and only its monuments remained in the middle of the square. The trees that danced in the wind, the green grass and partly trampled ...

The wooden stages set up hours earlier for artists to present themselves to the public and many other miserable people, who like him tried to take shelter under the various bandstands scattered throughout the place. The rainy region, even in the summer, had a defined time for the rains to fall. The population is already on the alert about this. At three o'clock in the afternoon, every day, it happens. It occurs in any season of the year. For this reason it is a fertile and productive land.

Leaning against the rail that surrounds the place where he sheltered from the strong storm that fell in the last hours of the day. He contemplated the void through which the many waters flowed.

And in a confused reflection he tried to understand something more about what was before his eyes. However, without being able to define exactly what was concrete or abstract.

That brilliant mind was chained within a nearly dead brain, he could not find the strength to describe the terrible evil that happened to him.

As an irrational being with little intelligence, he looked at so many things and seemed to see nothing or understand, he was perplexed by what only his dark imagination allowed him to see. The vision eroded by the decline of age and because of the health shaken by the mistreatment, he sometimes lacked.

It was common to stumble and fall during the long walks he used to do in search of survival. The shredded knees were the perfect proof of the extensive pilgrimage made to stay alive, although it makes little sense to him, even less to the world around him. It was just a stray. In his wanderings on that Sunday morning, he didn't dare stop in front of the buildings and skyscrapers located around the wide square. Because they had a tight garrison and the guards prevented any beggar from approaching the luxurious condominiums.

In an attempt to disturb the residents with their miseries. On one occasion he suffered aggression from one of them and he just didn't get beaten to death because popular people intervened and saved his skin.

So, since then, he tried to stay far away from that place. The avenue that passed right next to the square, and carried the same name as it, ended its long journey on the banks of the Guajara River.

Chapter 2 -See-O-Weight

There was Ver-O-Peso, where Luís spent most of his adolescence and met the one who adopted him two decades ago. The dying man went down the avenue, leaning against the curb to avoid being hit by the various vehicles traveling at high speed and making the environment too dangerous to move. He went to the port and outside the guardrail he could watch the ships that remained at anchor in the distance.

They unloaded their loads on ferries, while others continued on their way to different destinations. Despite all the confusion that obscured his mind, it was still possible to remember his origins, remember his past and know where he came from. Even through confused memories and full of unreadable points.

Which allowed him at that moment to observe the infinite on the muddy waters of the extensive river.

And to miss home, the old fishing father, the mother housewife. The other two brothers he left behind when he came to the capital and never wanted to see them again. Even after being adopted by Naomi and lived as a prince. Heir to untold fortune.

In complete disgrace he shed his tears for the emptiness he felt inside his chest and for understanding that it became impossible to rescue everything he left behind. With no family and friends to lean on, he felt like a shadow.

Someone who went unnoticed wherever he went, useless, whatever remains of what is thrown away. He continued to wander the streets, saw the marketers and their sales full of customers. They chose and bought everything.

He recalled the times when he arrived from the interior, aboard a fishing vessel, and made the place his home. The difference was that before he was in his prime, he was just a child and a flame of hope that burned inside his heart and that made him believe in a promising tomorrow. However, in the bitter present that was, everything had ceased to exist. His most intense dreams were shattered, they were suddenly canceled without him having a chance to try to avoid it. Who could be held responsible for what happened? Was it God or the Devil's fault for the damn madness that invaded his mind?

Who cursed him and made him that walking weirdo? What would he have done to deserve such punishment? Perhaps he was cursed for running away from home on that fishing vessel when he was ten years old. For coming to live in the big city without even saying goodbye to his family.

A divine rebuke for having acted so callously towards those who truly loved him as a son. is brother. Who knows the real reason, the truth was that the evil happened to him and nothing more could be done to correct such malignancy, he always wore the same broken clothes and a burlap sack that was grimy on his shoulders he went on, wandering the paths of the uncertain life he had left.

Small fishing boats were anchored at the pier, bringing many fish inside to supply the market. They sold everything very cheaply to middlemen who resold it at an absurd price to consumers. He looked from afar at what was happening around him, confused, he assimilated little. Watching the frantic movement and running at the fair.

Both the marketers and those who made varied purchases, according to their needs. Nobody noticed the presence of the dying man in those surroundings and that made it easier for him to put his hand in the merchant's bag of flour.

And in that way he ate a little, killing the hunger and longing for times gone by, when he could taste at will without having to hide. Fruits and vegetables were scattered on the floor, some spoiled and others in perfect condition that could be used for consumption and sometimes it was the only daily meal.

Just ahead there was another spot full of beggars similar to him and others scattered around the city. It was called the clock square. Due to a high pole made of concrete.

With a huge clock to guide the population of the time. While traveling in the shopping center, next to it was the city hall and the grain trade. There were a lot of dried fish, and the distribution of fresh fish. In addition to the Our Lady church, the Court of Justice and several clothing and appliance stores.

The place was very busy and visited by people from all walks of life, even by tourists who enjoyed the castle's fort. A tourist attraction from the times when people from Pará fought important battles against invaders.

Some cannons were still installed in the same location. Where the combatants faced their opponents and emerged victorious. And the merchant navy command headquarters was built right there. He liked to lie on the hard cement benches scattered in space.

Or leaning against the trunk of one of the thick hundred-year-old mango trees planted across the entire length of the place. On the roofs of the lower houses, a large number of vultures could be seen. Who were preparing like an army ready to attack and feed on the remains of dead fish.

They cleaned the garbage thrown away by the fishermen, the dry bank of the river located in the part where all types of landings were made. Also, there were other animals that were also decomposing and served as food for the birds.

Nobody was surprised until dark, when it arrived at night and each one needed a corner to sleep. Then the thing was dangerous, those who did not belong to the territory demarcated by the beggars of the area, should retire or risk even death.

Far from there, about five hundred meters away, you could see a very spacious street. Following it, he would arrive at his place of origin, where he could certainly rest from his labors. Important buildings were visible from the start.

Which deserved the attention of anyone passing by, On the right side was the imposing headquarters of the Pará Military Fire Brigade, where men committed to saving lives met.

Just ahead he came across the Brazilian Navy school of sailors. Full of young people aspiring to reach high posts in this segment of the country's armed forces. To the right of the long street, the State Academy of Letters was located.

Stage for the emergence of many highly important writers in the literary scene of Pará, and next to it was located the Peter in Oak school, a place where several personalities studied. As well as many of today's politicians, judges, lawyers. All other notable public figures.

And among them, he too, Luís Gustavo, who completed his secondary studies there and almost entered three of the most coveted colleges of the time. Without a doubt, he would guarantee his place in one of the chairs of the coveted literary world.

And it is a kind of space for people who stood out in society, in which he learned to live and admire, of course, if he were not mentally weak to the point of going crazy, for not enduring the emotion of the first of countless other victories that were deserved. Despite his immense intellectual capacity.

In the center of everything was another of the dozens of squares scattered in the great city of mango trees. The one with the flag had several masts with the three flags of the State. Place of celebrations on festive dates, however, when passing in front of such places he remembered nothing, there were few vague memories of what he was and who he had become. in today's world, it summed up only in a managed by the time that punished his appearance, transforming him into that decadent being, disgusting in the eyes of the beholder.

Perhaps in the past, if things had taken a different course, they would admire you for your intelligence and beauty. However, since his luck turned to bad luck and threw him into the pit, in constant dismay and what was left was to live like a mangy dog. whose filth was perceived in the distance. He was on his way to his resting place.

After all, the day was over and the darkness of the night was knocking on the doors. He needed to hurry up so as not to miss the point, if he weren't smart he would lose his sleeping place to another shirtless man who might be looking for a corner to lay his head on.

He followed the narrow Ó de Almeida street, always watching for signs before crossing the wide avenue, to finally reach his final destination. Even though it crosses the Riachuelo lane, the site of the various prostitution spots that housed all kinds of prostitutes and their despicable partners.

Addicts, thieves, murderers and all the city's rabble showed up there daily to satisfy their most shameful sexual instincts. A real focus of sexually transmitted diseases. Prostitutes sat on the high sidewalks in front of the brothels waiting for customers.

Lurking for those who happen to pass the street less than four meters wide. Wearing short skirts or tiny shorts, leaving your shame in plain view to pique men's interest. They were bold enough to offer themselves to programs and some of them went even further. They launched themselves at those who passed by, pulling any individual who approached from there, begging them to pay for a moment of pleasure.

Less clear, a dying man like him who had nothing to offer, not even good looks. Without taking into account the filth spread over your body for a long time without taking a good shower. His huge nails, full of dirt, the grating odor of the sticky wax on his body was felt from afar.

Teeth rotted from never being dug. Her long gray hair and full of lice. There were so many that they ran down to the yellowed, grown beard. Color caused by fun extracted from the smoke expelled from the smoke of an old pipe. In these conditions, he daily passed in that den of immoralities unnoticed.

Just like the sewage rats that occasionally crossed the alleys without anyone realizing that they existed. Finally it reached the end point of the journey. The avenue with little traffic, all stores and shops with closed doors. At the intersection the closed traffic light could be advanced by pedestrians without much haste.

Underneath a fine serene rain that undoubtedly was on its way. The deserted square gave way to the marginals on duty and their evils, to disputes between the dense darkness of the coming night. And the yellow lights from the various posts scattered on all sides contributed to the danger.

The gazebos were, as usual, crowded with miserable people lying on the floor on plastics, old newspapers or cardboard, but each one knew his space and his remained empty until he arrived.

He was very tired of the fatigue of yet another toil in search of survival, it was not easy to overcome adversity. Even though he lives like a raw animal, he almost doesn't realize the reality around him.

To help with the arrival of sleep, he drank a few sips of the favorite cachaça he always had on hand. It was like gasoline for a car in motion, if it were missing it would stop the engine, for the other less disturbed companions.

It would be possible to endure poverty and discouragement with drunkenness. Being constantly drunk to numb their minds and momentarily blind their understanding. For him, however, who lived in a part alien to almost everything in the real world, the strong drink served only to keep his energies and relax his tired body.

The human brain is a masterpiece of nature that, even if damaged, can still do many wonders, and with its eyes closed, falling into a deep sleep, the dying man began to dream.

Chapter 3 - Memories

If his mind was locked to the point of not assimilating reality, at least his subconscious could still bring through flash dreams of archived memories, and so he was able to go back in his childhood time, when beside Bernardo and Lucinda they bathed on the banks of the wide Guajará River, which was in the lower Amazon, with its muddy waters.

And strong currents capable of leading even the most resistant adult man, as well as the best swimmers to the bottom, causing the wreck of grandiose boats. However, with the adventurous courage of a child and the brothers were not afraid to have fun. Diving in the waves that came and went on the sand of the deserted beach.

There were many plants with edible fruits on the island, and they enjoyed everything they could find.

Mangoes of various species, jackfruit, cashews and top quality, guavas, diverse fruits, were a true paradise. But one day, after growing up and discovering that the world went beyond the banks of the river and the beauty of its waves, that besides the infinite waters there were many other things to be discovered and conquered.

So he decided to leave his family and all that natural beauty behind and flee into the unknown. He hitched a ride on the first fishing vessel that anchored a few days on the island, hiding in the hold, he managed to reach the capital and survive among the strangers without regretting the decision made. But, what is the result of having exchanged your humble life as a riverside for the adventure of going out into the world in search of adventures? He met a millionaire lady and at least for a while he enjoyed everything she offered him.

Without missing or missing what he left in his past, but finally came the divine rebuke that sent him to the bottom of that miserable pit. The dream was founded when the night darkness began to dissipate, in a few hours the dawn would say goodbye and the sun would enter the scene with all its brightness and rays.

Warming the coldness that brought comfort, after the heat that it had to endure the previous afternoon, during long walks. Unless, again, the black clouds of water prevented its clarity. If it rained again, as usual at that time of year.

In the month of carnival, people could already be seen partying in advance with costumes and drinking, those who were wealthy and did not mind throwing money away had fun in the small bars located in strategic places around.

The traditional bar in the square, which some time ago served as a meeting point for people intellectuals, where it became common to chat with the most important names in music. Also literature and arts in general, as well as the most respected public people of the time. But things changed and there was only an empty space of importance, full of drunks and rioters. He wandered around the place, confused, disturbed.

Totally disoriented. While most normal people were having fun, he and others like him paraded randomly like lost souls. Looking for someone who could give them something to eat. A couple approached Dona Rita's stall, she sold typical foods and they tasted delicious food, the poor devil, starving, just looked.

Perhaps his mediocre mind was no longer able to reason correctly, but he still knew how to identify the aroma and taste of food. Since she was a child, she loved that dish and would not easily forget it, Dona Maria, her mother, was an expert in preparing it.

And he delighted himself at will, until he was satisfied. Especially during the festivities of Our Lady of Perpetual Help. The patron saint, when dozens of the faithful attended the ceremony that took place every year. The pilgrimage began in the chapel, in the center of the village. Then he continued until he surrounded the entire route around the island and the crowd of pilgrims was immense, he loved to accompany the crowd, listening to their prayers and supplications to a dead saint, he knew that that statue could not hear them, but they believed in it. and there was no use trying to change the tradition. Naomi, her foster mother, was an unbelieving baby.

His parents as well as all his ancestors were, in addition to materialistic extremes, incorrigible atheists. But even though he came from a Catholic family, his faith was different. He believed in the existence of a God that no one could see, only feel. Alive and powerful who did not need someone to carry him on his shoulders in any kind of mess. That it was not made of clay, wood or plaster, but a spirit present everywhere. Well, that was his thought before it happened, before the mental disturbance reached him.

It didn't matter now, it didn't make sense anymore. They were just shadows that looked more like mists dissipated in the form of null and unreal thoughts. He approached the couple and, in the distance, filled his mouth with desire, wondering how tasty that typical food would be. Seasoned with plenty of pepper. Smoked bacon, pork feet and ears, in addition to the offal and all the seasoning traditionally used in the preparation.

It was not possible to resist the taste of that delicious regional dish. The young woman noticed the hungry man licking his lips with hunger and decided to buy a plate to give him. That he received and after he poured almost half a kilo of flour over it, he ate it desperately, as if he had been without food for days. The generous girl took pity on seeing him in that state, left the beggar with two more meals, guaranteeing him dinner and lunch the next day.

Merciful people, determined to reach out to help those who perished on the margins of society, did not always appear on the way. However, luck occasionally smiled at him and readied his pieces, helping or throwing him into the abyss.

Fate is the author of the story of each human being, his entire trajectory from beginning to end, along with his victories or failures, joys or sorrows. Laughter or tears. Everything is planned and calculated by him. And if something good or bad happens it comes from him, from his intentions for or against each one. It was up to the author of his story to write a useless beginning, a spectacular medium and at the same time terrible.

With a perhaps mediocre ending and in the worst possible way or, perhaps, surprising. The elderly man with gray hair and beard had dinner and sat on another late afternoon.

Watching the trees dance in the middle of the square where he lived, a cold wind blowing vertically from east to west of the place. Some people were walking. Some accompanied by their partners, couples in love, exchanging caresses, while others chose to parade alone. Others prefer to hold their pets' leash firmly. The grumpy observer saw everything in silence, inert like the statues and monuments found there and rarely noticed by those present, despite remaining before his eyes.

. There were long-shaped fruits, initially green and gray, when ripe, with a slightly yellow and sweet flavor, there were dozens of trees of the same fruit planted in the middle of the square. In the fall, a large number of fruits that fell on the grass could be harvested. They served as food for squirrels and for those who tried to survive at any cost

His gaze was fixed on everything that moved around him. Lovers holding hands, others embracing and exchanging caresses in some little place. There were those who, by choice or need, preferred to walk alone from side to side, some walking and others who ran like mad, in search of fulfilling so many dreams. There were also dog nannies circulating in the square who were paid by the rich only to walk for hours with their dear pets.

The animals were different from the others seen on the streets of the metropolis, chubby, their hair shone so clean, without any stains or dirt because they were treated well. Their owners spent a lot of money taking them to the vet, to the beauty salon to do a special treatment as if they were real people.

Some of the more daring even wore clothes and put shoes on animals as if they needed such things. Everything to snub the poorest and show the power they had.

For while throwing so much money out of the window with superfluous things, outside they died of hunger and cold and lack of care. Many unfortunates like him who had nothing, not even those who cared about their miserable state, even died on the sidewalks. The vast majority of Brazilians are selfish by nature. Also, just look at your roots and you will see that your attitudes make sense.

Coming from three races completely opposed to each other and with different ideals, where one dominated with rigor and disdain the other two weaker. And these, having fear, cowardice and naivety as characteristics, the end result of this merger could not be worse.

As in the colonial times of that land, the wealthiest and wealthiest people could still be seen showing their whips to the least favored menacing them to slavery. Luís Gustavo remained there, in the same place.

Sitting on the green grass of the square by the name of the republic, staring at what passed in front of him almost without batting an eye. I was not able to reason clearly. He understood very little what he saw and difficultly deciphered every image processed by his brain damaged by madness.

Birds flew from tree to tree, with their diverse and loud songs, as if they were a beautiful symphony. His ears heard the song clearly. However, little did they clearly assimilate the perfect musical notes contained in them. The children ran in a tireless game, seemed to be electric or powered by batteries that never ran out. They were beautiful, well cared for and fed the best.

They wore clothes and shoes from famous brands, even the color of their skin looked out of this world, whether white or black, they looked special.

It was not like the riverside boys raised on the banks of the Amazon rivers or in the slums, accustomed to eating wild fruits with fried fish or rice with dried meat and beans of the type that takes forever to cook. Right behind him was a tall statue made of cement and plaster, in the shape of a crowd of people with spears and swords in hand. It was a monument erected for the explorers who arrived in Pará and colonized the land.

The history of these people and their origins were impressive, their bold pride was already huge at that time, knowing that the existence of life in this part of Brazil is dated well before the arrival of the Portuguese.

As some archaeological findings have proved, the ancient inhabitants of Brazilian prehistory were divided into three groups, according to the way of life and the tools. Thus, the peoples emerged: hunter-gatherers, from the coast and farmers. These groups, later called by the European colonizers as Indians. Archaeological records have been found proving the human presence in the Lower Amazon archipelago since 3000 BC.

In the Lower Amazon, farmers lived in huts or underground houses. Since 3,500 years ago. These people knew about pottery, dyes, natural medicinal compounds. They practiced burning to clear the land and planted cassava. The best known culture of this group was ceramics, which had a peculiar decoration and size.

The period from 500 to 1300 was the height of culture in the Amazon. In high school, Luís was very knowledgeable in this regard, he knew everything about the history of his state and the entire region.

Other students paid to take private lessons with the young man who mastered the subject well. He often thought about becoming a historian, but due to the importance of the social environment where he lived alongside his adoptive mother, he decided to give his opinion on something more interesting.

However, at that moment none of that made any sense, how many times he passed in front of the same monument and made spectacular comments about its importance. Showing how great his knowledge on the subject was, and at that moment he could say nothing because his mind was blank.

Empty, endless uselessness. After twenty years in that sad situation, would he ever be rescued? Would he be seen in the gutter by any of the old friends with whom he shared so much knowledge in other times?

Did they ever walk through the square and contemplate their misery, without, however, having the courage to approach and at least mock their decadent situation? It was impossible to know for sure, but it didn't matter, because if it happened he didn't even notice. For hours he was in the same place, his eyes fixed on the landscape. As well as everything that moved, however without any great definition. A false laugh could be seen on his lips, partially covered by his bulky beard.

He seemed to be happy, satisfied with something, but it was only the mind-blowing effects of madness that gnawed at his brain. So he decided to get up a little and go in another direction. He was hungry and remembered the delicious typical foods that the girl gave him in the tent that was in front of the Theater. A beautiful mansion painted in blue.

Located right in the center of the square. Once there, the lady remembered him and served him. His hands were shaking a lot and he was barely able to steady his spoon in the food, it took a considerable time to feed.

A glass of juice accompanied the lunch which was on a whim. After thanking him for his kindness, he retired back to the gazebo where he slept. There he spent the night in the company of several others who were homeless. After removing the dirt and placing the burlap bag on the floor covered with white tiles.

Using it as a pillow, she lay down to get some rest. He took a sip of the cachaça he always carried by hand and whispered. Visitors entering the room were startled by the presence of the beggar.

And immediately they left there differently from what happened before their complete decay, when he still had the title of heir to the lady of rubber, he had many privileges now lost. frequented only fine and refined environments. Their friendships were handpicked and belonged to the highest point of society.

And several were the girls from good families who wished to have at least some of their valuable attention. There were often disputes between the candidates for dating and the daughter of the then mayor of Belem. She who was part of his select group of friends. And with whom he has been making out a few times, he wanted to be his wife, which he in no way insisted on. Now, after you have turned it three hundred and sixty degrees, look what happened. He became a disgusting being to everyone who saw him in that deplorable state. Would Juliana, the former suitor, recognize him if she saw him? Certainly not, she lost the joviality that won her over and only the most horrendous side remained. And macabre. He was sleeping soundly.

Snoring like a pig and stank like a skunk, no one could bear to stay by his side. This was due to the bad odor that came out of his fetid body, except for those similar to him. He woke up after a few hours of sleep and it was already mid afternoon that day. As always, there was a strong wind, announcing the arrival of rain that usually falls at the same time.

The sun disappeared from the sky and in its place the water-laden clouds darkened the entire city. With the swaying of its branches, the trees dropped ripe fruit and several people took the opportunity to gather them, many other starving people were among the harvesters, from a distance he just admired everything in silence.

He was not given to make verbal comments, he hardly spoke, just what was necessary and when necessary. The frequent thunderstorms and lightning accompanied the beginning of the flood that falls incessantly, wetting everywhere and creating small puddles of mud.

The square, which had been crowded with visitors from an early age, soon emptied completely, no sign of a living soul could be seen. Only at dusk did he stop thunderstorms. And the charged clouds dissipated. The storm ceased and the usual cold remained. That intense climate that made the shirtless teeth chatter during the early hours. Luís Gustavo was part of that number of discouraged, homeless and without any comfort. From where he stood he looked up, looked at the buildings, buildings around. He knew that the millionaires who lived outside the storm that had stopped minutes ago lived there. For they lived locked in their luxurious apartments. surrounded by so much luxury that it prevented them from perceiving what was happening outside their fortified rooms.

When they lay on their beds, they covered themselves with their expensive duvets, thin covers and heated up to satisfy their intentions, how much antagonism, while some eat and drink satisfactorily, others feel their stomachs bite inside. Some have too much, others too little and there are still those who have nothing. Is that justice?

Is God really fair to his creatures? The unfortunate man who lived in the square, like everyone else, was once a practicing Christian and firmly believed in divine justice. In fact, he used to think that his good life was the result of the rewards for his efforts.

For the faith he had in a higher being, and he believed that he even fell from grace. Their faith, however, was not based on customary idolatry. Your parents and the rest of the family. As well as the inhabitants of the island where he was born, they were fervent Catholics and followed their traditions to the letter. However, he loved the long processions in the festivities of the saint, but it was only the agony of a boy, after all he had no confidence in her. Even in the thought of a child, born in the bush, like an Indian.

It was possible to analyze that something lifeless is dead and the dead can do nothing. Therefore, statues could not hear him or answer his prayers, he saw God in nature. He would sit for hours near the waterfall in a stream near the house, watching the waters flow towards the river. The tall, low vegetation, the enchanting green, listening to the birds' whistling, the nightingale.

The wheezing, the toucan with its huge beak. The heron that caught small fish on the banks of the stream, capuchin monkeys jumping from one branch to another.

The laziness that took an immense amount of time to reach the top of the tree, everything was so beautiful and charming, in his childlike way of thinking, that was God, the creator of all things. But worse for him if he expressed this reasoning to anyone, he would be criticized and could take a beating like that, in their view he would be blaspheming. Dishonoring what was most sacred. The Lady Judith was a Roman Catholic and did not admit heresies.

If someone spoke badly of his little saint, he would jump down and shout "look at the respect!". A true defender of the faith in Our Lady of Nazareth. When he came to the capital and lived for a few years at Ver-o-Peso, during the pilgrimage he used to accompany the fluvial candle just to be able to ride the boats for free.

And eat for free the delicacies that were distributed. Later, when the procession went on foot through the city streets. He mixed with the crowd. He made a lot of mixes as a form of entertainment, he even pulled such a payment rope from his promises, but it was pure fun. When he went to live with Naomi, he left the damage and was educated to behave decently.

As it actually demanded the society of which it would be part. He learned correctly how to have good manners, to act elegantly with the proper class that his new condition demanded. Dalí onwards was obliged to attend Mass every Sunday and perform all the prayers the priest ordered. He was confirmed and made all the communions of the Blessed Sacrament. He became a complete Christian in the eyes of the church and his mother. But what was the point of so much belief in mission or that if in the end neither the plaster saint nor God helped him? If they were not able to prevent such unhappiness?

Well, what good would it do to ask whether or not there was justice in divine decisions if for poor devils like him and his companions in misfortune it all came down to endless hell? The truth is that his world has collapsed, has been reduced to ashes and was nothing more than a figure. A shadow lost among other shadows of so many worthless lives.

These truths remained beyond his demented imagination, only the very destiny that condemned him to live in vegetation remained narrating his sad story while amusing himself with his intense failure. The silence was interrupted by the shrill noise of an accident. It was something very serious that had just happened on the avenue nearby.

A beggar crossed the traffic light and was taken by surprise in the middle of the road. It crashed on the asphalt about a hundred meters from the crash site. Several onlookers went to see the disfigured body that remained stretched there for a long time until the deceased popes decided to appear.

He was nothing more than a pauper, without a name or whoever claimed his filthy body. He looked at Geraldo's deplorable state, all shattered on the track and pool of blood that was dripping from him. The despicable way in which he was treated by those who should show a little solidarity at least at the time of death. But without money in his pocket and a name at the top of the social list he would be treated with contempt, worse than a garbage bag like the one he carried on his shoulders.

Despite the obscure mind it was possible to understand immediately that it would have the same end. After all, what was different about the other losers who lived in the square? Geraldo was a good man, he progressed during his youth as a realtor. Becoming the owner of the largest company in this industry before the age of thirty-five.

And his fame exceeded the limits of his expectations. It would have been the biggest icon in this segment, if its partners had not used extreme ambitions and taken it to the last penny.

Throwing him into the deepest ditch of debt ever seen, which made him lose to the roof where he took shelter. Bankrupt and without new perspectives, he sank into drunkenness, becoming drunk. The wife abandoned him and his children felt ashamed of what the father had become and, alone, in complete poverty, without being able to work and maintain his own livelihood ended up on the streets.

Like one more on the growing list of indigents. He was her sleeping companion in the square bandstand. They exchanged no more than a dozen words a year, but I still had him as a friend. The day they talked the most was when they met and he told his story. After that, the silence became an almost impassable wall between the two. After Geraldo's departure, loneliness completely occupied his limited world.

He was the only one who trusted to exchange two words. Now it was just him and the confused thoughts that always plagued him. The center of criminal expertise took the body of the deceased to the autopsy, from there it would go to the crematorium and his family. This is the end reserved for frets like him, with no value. And what about him, would there be someone who, at such a sorry moment, would appear to claim the deceased and bury him with more dignity? Of course not.

His parents whom he dared to abandon, nor the adoptive mother who once gave him a valuable surname. None of them would be at their mediocre funeral, there for the suburban bands, public cemetery and low quality.

Always with open doors for anyone the devil decided to take to the beyond. Or, who knows, to see the smoke from his bones burning in the public crematorium, as happened with the hit friend, but it was not yet the right time to be concerned with such detail

Chapter 4 - Meeting

At forty years of age, twenty of them maddened and looking like a man in his sixties, he still had the strength to continue on the damn journey as a beggar for alms and so would his journey towards an uncertain and suffering future. He had no illusions that happiness would smile again, perhaps luck had already smiled enough and exhausted all opportunities.

After all, it is not routine for good ladies and millionaires to appear, wanting to adopt poor people, especially when dealing with a grumpy old man. That morning he followed the usual route and crossed the main avenue of the shopping center.

When he came across several luxury cars that parked in front of one of the most exquisite hotels. Frequented by great personalities, he intuitively decided to stop and observe who the celebrity would be arriving at the place. The woman was expressive in appearance. She wore a long red dress with an opening on the side of her right leg, stepping firmly on high, thin heels. he gets out of the vehicle and headed for the hotel entrance. Followed closely by huge security guards that looked more like four concrete walls around her. Ensuring you total protection. The distance between her and her observer was only about four meters.

And her eyes, even cloudy from the large amount of alcohol she had ingested minutes before and from the mental confusion that continually confused her reason, it was possible to identify her. The passing of time did not change the lady of rubber, which was still stunning. His sixties and fifties did not seem to exist, he appeared to be in his late thirties when he adopted him. The beauty of the powerful woman remained intact, it was the miracles that money could do.

She disappears in the elevator that would take her to her destination, perhaps to the penthouse or to the casino, would meet with other businessmen in one of the several existing suites, or simply seek to rest from her numerous commitments. Him, outside and with no chance of entering the place to try to get closer.

I could still remember her routine, even in a blurry way. His heart sped up at the sight of her. That feeling could not be confused with a normal attitude of someone who naturally sees a friend or a distant relative.

Crazy people would never act naturally. What happened there was pure instinct, like a pet that after being abandoned for several months or years to see its owner again and is able to recognize him. Luís Gustavo recognized Naomi, despite his insanity.

From that moment on, he remained around the building, trying to review it. It couldn't get too close, the environment was frequented by people belonging to the social elite, the garrison was permanent. But nothing prevented him from staying around, watching, and he did. It was forty-eight hours of waiting, she really came to rest. Certainly on the roof, where the pool was. Sipping your favorite whiskey, accompanied with some ice cubes.

How could the troubled beggar understand so much about his preferences and the place she chose to relax? Well, in the past he has also had the pleasure of accompanying you on one of those five-star tours. And she took a bath in the treated waters of the same pool where at that moment the millionaire was cooling. And despite being left behind.

Losing the right and the opportunity to continue with such privileges could still flash with fond memories. A little of everything he lived was left in his fragile memory. Perhaps it was this that awakened in him the instinct to approach and see more closely that woman who somehow brought him embarrassing, confused memories, but accompanied by longing.

She got in the car and went on her way without even realizing that very close to where she spent so much time relaxing was the one she once loved. As a son he gave a home and planned to give his entire fortune. His life, since he gave up fighting to heal the future heir, has not been the same. She deceived everyone who admired her and the critics with a fanciful story. The question that did not want to remain silent in the heavy conscience of the heiress of Guimarães Velasco was why he had given up on Luís Gustavo.

Every night she had insomnia, she even had nightmares without finding answers to this question that brought her strong concerns. She was a woman of many means, medicine and scientific knowledge only increased. No doubt, with a little more effort and determination.

He would have found a way to treat his son. Any other mother would have shown more compassion instead of abandoning him to his own devices in an asylum for the mentally ill.

In a conversation with Lucy, after confessing the terrible act committed to her best friend, there were several questions:

— And after the psychiatric hospital was closed, what destiny did the poor man have?

— Honestly, my friend, I'm not sure

— But you didn't even go looking for him, didn't you realize that you left him in a city without relatives, lost to strangers?

— I must confess that it hurt me so much to make such a decision, but, being a woman with such social prestige, how could I continue living with a mentally insane person in my house? It was the only way out to tell everyone that Luís Gustavo was dead

— Naomi, my friend, you deceived us all with that barbaric lie, even made us go to a false funeral, I shed many tears myself, because I loved him as if he were a true nephew. This is not done, it is cruel to all those who love and respect you!

— I know, that's why I'm here revealing my mistake and asking you to forgive me

— Sorry, we have been friends since our childhood, I have deep affection for you. But I feel that I will never be able to forget what you did to me and the harm done against that poor boy, abandoning him as if he were a dog without an owner and forging his death, while the poor fellow was kept inside a psychiatric ward, treated with the worst tortures, as we well know.

— But what could I do about it, my friend.

Make it public that my heir has completely lost his mental balance and would be a madman who would be betting the fate of all my fortune?

— No, show a little more sensitivity and invest all available resources in the search for a cure and fulfill your duty as a mother, protecting you at the moment when he most needed your compassion! But what did you do instead? He preferred to defend the good name of the Velasco and throw the poor devil into a dungeon, hiding from society that his choice had been a fiasco. That the boy harvested at the Ver-O-Peso fair was a seed that really did not succeed, as many opponents said it would be?

— Yes it's true. I admit that that was the main reason that led me to make such a decision. When I adopted Luís, I was really criticized by people who said it was a mistake to adopt a street boy to give him the important name of my family, but I was pedantic and insisted on saying that I had done the right thing and that later on I would prove it. to all who dared to contradict me. And my boy's approval in the three most competitive colleges in this state would be the moment to pass this great victory on their faces, but unfortunately he was so badly affected and the only thing left for me was shame and humiliation. I tried to find a cure, we went abroad, but all in vain. So I had no choice, I forged his death

— But what evil, did you prefer to sacrifice it than having to listen to the scorns of your opponents?

— Yes, friend, I was extremely cowardly

— I feel sorry for you

Naomi, and at the same time ashamed of your insane attitudes. I'm not sure which of the two is the most mentally disturbed, whether he or you

— I thought I could count on your understanding

— How can I understand such malice, aware that my nephew was thrown into the gutter and today he may be dead or wandering around like a João, who knows where? No, I cannot forgive or understand such a lack of love for your fellow man!

From that day on, the friendship between the two women came to an end and Lucy never wanted any kind of contact with Naomi again. During meetings at parties and social gatherings, he avoided any approach. And she made a point of revealing to everyone else on the same level what the insensitive businesswoman had done to her own son, who she adopted some time ago.

It did this in order to maintain its prestige in the face of the social lights that illuminate the most powerful, and with that it caused the contempt on the part of those who were touched by such perversity to fall on it. A journalist, belonging to an important local media group, decided to investigate further the story of the young heir who was left in the open by the then businesswoman. Its main objective was to publish in detail a book with the true destiny of the poor boy who passed from heir to the rubber lords. Who became a pauper, mercilessly abandoned on the streets of the city of Belem do Pará when he completely lost his mind.

This would undoubtedly not only be the biggest journalistic scoop hitherto seen, but also the most exciting literary work ever published. Naomi, aware that Lucy had not kept her secret, was indignant and apprehensive about the scandal that would certainly happen. It didn't take long for comments to appear in local magazines and gossip columns, as well as in the social realm of which he was a part.

Groups of people dedicated to defending humanitarian rights began to criticize the businesswoman indirectly. And it was already rumored that they were planning to gather a crowd in a march through the city center. To protest the inhumane act practiced by the millionaire against Luís Gustavo. The popular revolt over complaints made against the owner increases daily. Especially from most of the big companies in the state, which went from simple stores to banks,

In addition to gas stations, clinics, transporters, and several others, it made her become a recluse inside her own home. Aware that all that sudden repudiation originated from the indiscretion of Lucia, in whom she would have trusted her greatest secret.

He was very angry and made yet another of his thoughtless decisions to try to prevent his traditional name and that of his family from falling into complete disgrace. He summoned one of his most loyal employees to carry out an immediate mission, giving him strict orders:

— Remember, Mr. Matias, that unfortunate woman must pay a high price for what she did to me and to the valiant name of my family. Take the utmost care that everything goes as planned, so that there are no mistakes

— You can leave it, lady, that unhappy person will never find her tongue in her teeth again

— Very well, then go and perfectly execute the plan we have outlined. And don't forget, Mr. Matias, without fail!

— Leave it to me!

The mistress's orders were for the gunslinger to commit a crime on demand. Lucia, for having publicly denounced her old friend, should be killed. But so that the name of the assassin was not involved in what happened. Matias was a professional matador and was hired to perform the job.

That he would have already murdered many of his boss's foes. If so, then that would be just more among so many others. Lucy was a renowned doctor and owner of an aesthetic clinic located in a privileged area of the capital.

That late afternoon she intends to return home and drives her car along one of the several avenues, all with traffic totally bottled up. It was after twenty o'clock and she remained trapped among dozens of other vehicles, unable to find a way forward. Matias, two more of his subordinates were waiting for her at the intersection two kilometers away. Knowledge of the model and license plate of the car, in addition to the exact location of your residence.

As soon as she reached the vicinity of the luxurious condominium where she lived, she was followed closely by the criminals. They approached her before she even went through the electronic gate, six accurate pistol shots were fired that culminated in the doctor's death. The marginals left the place after confirming the death.

The police started to investigate the causes of the crime, with characteristics of settlement of accounts. The attack that seemed to have been perfect caught the attention of the population. He immediately became suspicious of the great coincidence between the complaints. That were done by the victim and his murder, the news commented on the episode.

And the most daring cast suspicion on the businesswoman Naomi Velasco, as being the mastermind of the heinous crime. People of all ages paraded that Saturday morning through the streets. They followed the avenues of the capital of Pará, demanding that justice be done and the guilty be punished.

While the crowd demanded that the authorities take the necessary steps, the filthy beggar walked among them. Without realizing that he was the same man abandoned decades ago by the millionaire, after going crazy. He was the reason why Lucia had been murdered by Naomi. For she would have discovered that her death was nothing more than a farce forged by the murderer, in order to hide her mistakes.

Unhappy with the friend's attitudes towards her son, when he became an invalid. Due to the madness that destroyed part of his mental health. She was the one who denounced the neglect and abandonment of the poor young man, at that time already a man of forty years.

And it tarnished the good reputation that that woman enjoyed in the society of Pará, seen as an example of love and mercy for needy friends. For Naomi, to mask her true soulless and ruthless personality, unable to think of the greater good. Seeking only the fruits of its actions for itself, it was the largest donor of funds to orphanages and charities.

Passing to society the idea of being a person totally concerned with the similar. With the denunciations made, all this farce fell to the ground and ignited the wrath of the facets who ordered the cowardly death of the doctor. Like any garbage residue exposed on the floor and which was trampled indifferently by the demonstrators, even so it was the poor devil, nobody noticed his presence. And he, too, did not understand why so much trouble. The claims made by the crowd meant nothing to the hungry. That he just wanted to find something to eat.

In fact, what their twisted mentality could understand was that they were getting in the way of people coming and going, that is, it became impossible to beg for alms during the long march. With the demands of the masses of people for the authorities to give a positive answer about the crime committed days ago, there was no other way than to summon the millionaire to testify about such accusations. Of course, in this country, the powerful never commit crimes and are always innocent, accompanied by half a dozen of the best lawyers she attended for only half an hour at the police station.

And her defenders exchanged a few words with the deputy who dismissed her without much detail. Under the protest of a tumultuous crowd, she left protected by several security guards. Then he returns to the mansion where he lived. Completely free of all charges, impunity once again prevented justice from actually being served against the guilty. The murdered doctor's relatives were outraged at the infamous way the authorities handled the case. And they sought resources from all sides to condemn the criminal, however. Without hard evidence and witnesses to support the allegations made, it was all a tremendous waste of time. The millionaire won again.

Chapter 5 --The Interview

Marilda Campos was an excellent journalist, widely recognized in the social environment in which she lived, a competent professional and took her work very seriously. In view of the news, the possibility that the heir of Guimarães Velasco is still alive and the whole story about his supposed death was nothing more than a farce created to hide the true condition in which he found himself. He had the unfortunate idea of investigating thoroughly and with that he ended up buying himself serious problems.

Putting her own life and that of the others she loved at risk. She followed clues that led her to the beginning of everything. Since Luís Gustavo passed the Faculty of Medicine and Engineering Law at the Federal University of Pará and two other private higher education institutions. Even when the candidate for the vacancies suffered a terrible mental breakdown, losing his mind.

Being unable to continue with academic training, according to the information found in the archives documents of these institutions. The patient was taken for psychiatric treatment by a family member of an unspecified name and never returned to claim his approval. Marilda, always keen on her goals, continued her investigations in order to discover the whereabouts of the alleged dead man. Since the evidence said he is still alive somewhere in that huge city.

He expanded his search for psychiatric hospitals in the hope of finding a professional in the field who could give any information that would help to elucidate the case.

And, after so many comings and goings, he met Joana Darc, a fifty-five-year-old lady who at the time was a nurse in one of the wings of the former mental hospital Julian Moreira. She and others were responsible for caring for patients who went through those types of monstrous therapies, as she described:

— There, my daughter, it was a sadness only to see those poor things receiving electric shock discharges every day, on the excuse that it would help to cure their madness. Wants to know? They stayed were even more crazy

— And did you witness everything up close?

— Yes, my daughter, very close, with nothing to do to help them

— And who gave the order for patients to be treated with all this cruelty?

— Now, girl, the doctors! They were the ones who determined who, how and when crazy people should receive shock treatment

— And do you remember the name of any of those patients who lived in that wing where you worked, Dona Joana?

— Why, and how could you forget, creature? Of course, I remember the names of all the patients I took care of. We live together for a long time, we form a type of family

— Great! Then tell me: Did you know a young man of about twenty two to twenty five years, by the name Luís Gustavo?

— This is Gustavo who freaked out after passing the entrance exam? But of course, my daughter, I do remember that poor boy

— Very well, then tell me everything to remember about this patient

— Well, what we found out was that he belonged to a very chic family, he was adopted as the only child of a millionaire. Known as the rubber tree, because it came from the lineage of former rubber plantation owners in the Amazon. And after the poor boy went crazy she put him in a madhouse, abandoning the poor devil. She never came back to see if the poor thing was still alive.

— Lady Joana, tell me: How many years do you think this patient remained hospitalized as an indigent after he was left in that hospital?

— Look, I still worked there for fifteen years, taking care of them and only leaves after the hospital closes

— And he stayed there all this time?

— Yes, nobody was released.

It was only after the government decided to extinguish the psychiatric treatment unit that they were all thrown onto the streets.

— Right. So, taking into account that he was admitted to the hospital in the age group that I described earlier, it is possible that he is under fifty years old, right?

— Yes, if you are still alive you should have a maximum of forty-five

— Perfect, Lady Joana, thank you very much for your valuable attention. I am grateful for the information provided for my research

— It was my pleasure to be able to help, my daughter

Journalist Marilda Campos already had enough evidence and information to start the search for the missing person, everything indicated that Luís Gustavo would be wandering the streets and she intended to find him. The most difficult part would be to identify him among so many other beggars around the city, especially considering his current appearance, completely changed from what it was twenty years ago.

He started to drive around in his car everywhere, hoping to locate him. It would be like looking for a needle in a haystack. It was almost impossible, but with persistence it would certainly succeed. He gave full priority to areas of greater agglomeration of beggars, such as street markets and plazas, where they usually went to order food and gathered to rest from their daily labors. In none of the plazas visited until then. It was successful, leaving only the largest to end the tireless search. President Vargas was the largest and busiest of all the other public squares in Belem.

Frequented by all types of people from different social strata. Due to the exuberant beauty through its historical monuments. The century-old fruit trees. The space reserved for leisure and the wide choice of attractions present there. It happened every weekend for the entertainment of its visitors. If the dying man were still alive and out in the open he would certainly be in that place. She began to patiently interview all the dying that she thought fit the created profile.

From the information collected from the nurse. It took age and physical appearance into account. Some were so confused in their minds that any dialogue was impossible.

Already discouraged, after so many unsuccessful attempts, she sat down on one of the several benches of raw cement existing in the square's square, carrying a brown leather bag, a camera, a small voice recorder, the pad of paper with staff and a pen to write down the observations.

And unexpectedly he noticed some of the homeless people gathered in a bandstand about a hundred meters ahead. With a leap he headed towards the place in the hope of finally completing his search for the pauper.

When he arrived there, he found several abandoned people sitting on the ground, eating ripe fruits that fell from the trees during the strong wind that had occurred hours before. On the right side of the room was a man lying on paper bags and a bag full of filthy things beside him. From what he saw in the others, none of them fit Luís's description. So he chose to wait for the elderly person to wake up to interview him. With the arrival of the stranger, the beggars got scared and ran away, she remained waiting to put the plan into practice.

Several hours passed before he woke up, but she waited for him. The unfortunate man finally wakes up and finds the beautiful woman watching him. At first he was surprised by what he saw, but then he retired without paying any attention to the one who was watching him. Marilda then decides to intervene and holds him by the old shirt, the previously white fabric was immensely stained, with a large, almost imperceptible sticker from the Holy Virgin.

The sticker was stamped on the front of his shirt, which he was given during the Nazareth candle festivities months ago. He turns to face seriously the one who dared to hinder his walk and gets caught looking at those beautiful blue eyes. She politely asks me to allow you a few minutes of attention.

He fulfills the request and in a few minutes they are already talking amicably as if they were old acquaintances. She used a strategy to capture the interviewee's interest. With assimilable subjects like talking about the square and the natural beauty that existed in it

He reasoned with great difficulty, but he was able, however, to understand what the beautiful girl with the colorful eyes said to him and clearly answered his questions.

Because he lived there for several years and knew everything about the place. Gradually the conversation became more interesting to the point where Marilda began to investigate the origins of the elderly, making him remember the past.

There was some difficulty, little clarity of memories and a confusion of disconnected ideas, but little by little she gathered important details until she concluded that in fact this was the man she had been looking for.

After taking him to the stall selling typical foods and paying the new friend a delicious meal, the journalist says goodbye to him. Entering an agreement that I would continue to visit him every day so that they could talk. In return she would always guarantee you another delicious new lunch like that.

He happily agreed with the proposal, after all, it was the guarantee of guaranteed daily food, who would refuse such an offer? In the days that followed, the two kept the routine meeting and the conversation, despite developing very slowly, brought positive results.

She was already sure of her convictions. Undoubtedly, that poor devil was the former heir of the rubber lords, however, he wanted to know more about the complete madness until the very moment they met. All the difficulties faced. Suffering in the asylum, torture and abandonment, but how would he go into detail on such a vast subject with stunted memory?

Crazed and without a clue about reality? At first, when he was victimized by the almost total loss of consciousness. Luís Gustavo was taken to the presence of the greatest professionals in the field of psychiatric treatment in the country, even abroad. But nothing could be done to restore his mental health, due to the delay in medicine in that particular field.

However, over two decades, progress has been significant. Other methods have been devised to resolve certain mental disorders. Causing the terrible treatment of electric shock to be abandoned. Marilda, after weeks without success in the interviews, decided to seek more information about the advancement of science to recover from mental atrophies.

And discovered that there was a possibility to revert Luís's current situation while she could send him to the South of the country and intern you at one of the clinics specializing in the subject.

As long as it could pay for the required dispersed highs, of course, that would be the biggest obstacle. She was a very prominent journalist in one of the major newspapers in the capital. However, his low salary did not provide him with the necessary conditions to afford spent sizes. It was there that he had the idea of looking for Alessandra Arrais, an old friend from university times. They graduated together at the same time, she in journalism and her friend in law. Despite following different paths, they maintained close ties.

And the friendship lasted for decades, later Alessandra won the title of excellent Law Judge and then held an important position in the State Court of Justice.

Becoming an interesting personality in the social context of Pará. The visit of the friend, after some time away, was received with great joy and the two exchanged confidences. They recalled good moments experienced in the past, finally, the journalist reveals the magistrate the real reason for her visit, explaining in detail the result of her research and exposing all the concrete evidence found during the investigation.

Alessandra, who was one of the greatest opponents of the rubber lady, not only because she understood that her attitude as a good Samaritan was nothing more than a mask that should be thrown to the ground. As if he understood that the entire Velasco heritage had been acquired unworthily.

Through the exploitation of the poor families of the rubber tappers who worked day and night in exchange for a miserable salary, while the bosses were getting rich. The judge's interest in the case delighted Marilda, who clarified the importance of restoring Luís Gustavo's mind in order to help him remember his entire history.

And using her as the main witness against Naomi, completely destroying her prestige and empire, Alessandra was a woman of many possessions and influences. With that I could easily get a place in one of the many private hospitals for the modern treatment of mental disorders in São Paulo. And their perspectives on this were not wrong, it happened exactly as planned.

The beggar was finally rescued and a project put into action. After having lived for five long years as a pauper in the square, he was taken to the city of São Paulo. and admitted to the largest and most requested psychiatric hospital in the country, there good professionals spent all their time trying to restore his conscience.

Of course, it would be a very difficult task, due to long periods in which he was exposed to the disease and his brain disconnected from the outside world, totally alienated from reality.

However, according to the results of the preliminary exams, cure was possible. There were great chances of recovering a good part of his memory and returning memories and memories that would help him to update himself in the present, with the possibility of recovering his consciousness almost completely. This declaration by the specialists brought greater hope to Marilda, who was looking forward to clarifying the whole truth involved in the life of that unfortunate man.

Luís was hospitalized under intense treatment for six months in the city without receiving any visit. Only after this period was he allowed to keep in touch with people other than the medical team that assisted him. The room to receive visitors was spacious and very comfortable.

Marilda stayed there for a few minutes until the patient was allowed to go to the place. The man who approached her in the company of a nurse looked strange, wearing clean clothes with trimmed hair and beard and looking several years younger.

He approached and as he sat in the black leather chair everything he admired. He looked into his blue eyes and smiled broadly. Honestly, she was unable to recognize him and expressed a dull, yellowish laugh. As if she were in a bad situation. Then, realizing the timidity of the visit, he extended his hand and announced his name:

— Hi, I'm Luís Gustavo, very pleased

She was astonished by the statement of the elegant young man who remained smiling in front of her, and timidly responded to the kindness, extending his hand to greet him:

— The pleasure is mine! I can't believe being yourself, how can it be possible?

— Sorry, have we met before?

— Don't you really remember me?

— No, it would be impossible to forget such beautiful eyes.

I was told that someone wanted to talk to me and I came to see who it was, but I don't remember seeing her before, I'm sorry

— I see, and what do you remember about your life?

— Everything but meeting you

— Interesting

— What would be so interesting that I remember everything about me and not you? Tell me, where do we meet from?

— My name Marilda Campos. I am a journalist and the person responsible for your admission to this hospital

— Sorry, but the last memory I have is that I was admitted to a psychiatric ward by my mother, years ago and never saw her again. I seem to have awakened from a deep sleep or a nightmare, everything is still a little confusing for me

— Remember your name?

— Yes, Luís Gustavo, only heir to Naomi Guimarães Velasco, aka rubber lady

— And what is your last memory of contact with your mother?

— I clearly remember everything until I was admitted to the psychiatric hospital. However, what happened over the years comes to mind in fragments

Luís's answer left the journalist astonished by the miracle made by God, through medicine, in the life of that man who seemed to have no solution any more.

Madness - Fiction Romance

There was the old dying man in the square, completely restored from madness, which almost completely destroyed his perception of reality, keeping him trapped in a dark world for so long. Despite the good results, it was decided that the patient would remain hospitalized under observation, the medical team continued with the evaluation for another six months, to ensure a more reliable recovery.

Twelve months later, after starting treatment, he was finally released and taken home. As he had no fixed residence. Marilda hosted him at his residence to be able to follow the evolution of his recovery closely. There was no need to hurry, everything should flow naturally. They went out, had dinner and went to the cinema. on several occasions the two passed by the president Vargas square. And he was thrilled to remember the five years spent there in total abandonment.

The filthy clothes he wore, the scraps of food taken from the garbage cans in front of the luxurious condominiums, where he was brutally treated several times. At his request, she took him to Ver-O-Peso to quench his longing for the times when he lived there as an assistant to marketers. Gradually and with the help of the new friend.

He was gradually recovering his memory and his memories became more real and complete. He could even remember small details from his past, previously forgotten in the darkness of the madness in which he was lost, for twenty years. They talked in the early hours in search of trying to go deeper into the details. Those who perhaps remained hidden in his subconscious. This therapy contributed a lot to better consolidate the ideas that little by little appeared and made him stay in tune with the present facts. While he rediscovered himself and definitively left that unreal world in which he lived penitent for two decades.

She wrote down all his evolutions and created an extraordinary story to be told to future generations. Alessandra, as always in a hurry, wanted to publicly reveal what had happened. Show population the true face of the supposed defender of the underprivileged and guardian of the less favored. Its greatest purpose was to unmask the lady of rubber.

And collapse your empire of deceit and lies. Especially at that moment when she intended to participate in the next political election. Running for state government. If, in addition to the influence he already had in society, he occupied the government, what limit of power would he have in his hands.

And what could she do against those who, like her and the murdered doctor, were opposed to her unjust and corrupt acts? Naomi was no different from her ancestors. They all got rich at the expense of exploiting people in need. Those willing to do anything to acquire a portion of food to give to their children, who, like them, would grow up in the bush like animals.

To later serve as cold buoys in the rubber plantations, harvesting the rich product that would enrich their masters. The times of rubber plantations have passed, modernity has arrived and it has become difficult to maintain slave labor, exploiting such families, paying the worker's sweat with food dishes.

However, nothing would prevent her from using other methods, even the most conventional ones, to achieve her unscrupulous goals. Trying to prevent it from happening in any way should be the main mission of the judge and all of her allies.

It was election year and the damn killer was among the candidates most likely to go to the second. shift. It was necessary that they take advantage of that electoral period to get all the dirt stored under the carpet on it.

Chapter 6 - The Trial

Judge Alessandra joined forces with her former college friend to devise a plan to bring down the candidacy of millionaire Naomi Velasco. The two had been enemies for many years and the disagreement between them would have been highlighted in some local newspapers and gossip magazines.

The dislike between them was reciprocal and known to all, there were only a few months to go before the elections and there could not be a more ideal time to spread mud on the fan and completely tarnish the candidate's reputed name in front of her voters.

The main weapon that would be used to denigrate the businesswoman's image sought to reveal to the whole society the farce created, the false story surrounding the supposed death of her adopted son, Luís Gustavo. Declared dead by the same twenty years ago during a tragic car accident, when in fact he remained alive.

In complete abandonment through the streets of the city, sleeping in the open after years in a hospital for the mentally ill. Without counting on any help on your part. The main idea would be to file a complaint through the local media and then take the case to court.

From there Alessandra would act as the magistrate responsible for judging the case, counting, of course, with the support of the left parties interested in preventing the opponent's rise.

Along with a large number of other authorities dissatisfied with the businesswoman. This was due to his abuse of power, because of the high social position he held. One month before the end of the elections, the newspaper Amazon bugle prints on the front page the photo of the Velasco family heir, supposedly dead two decades ago, in perfect health.

This was the title of the most widely read news story. And that caused the biggest stir in the city on the eve of the choice of the new government, he asked the readers if in fact Luís Gustavo was dead.

The article written by journalist Marilda Campos stated that everything was nothing more than a shameful setup by the millionaire and that the young man, now twenty years older, would not have died and was in good shape. Faced with serious accusations, the Regional Electoral Court decided to veto Naomi's candidacy.

This would happen immediately, if it did not provide clarification to society about what would be reported in the press. Despite her lawyers and the party she was affiliated with trying to prove in every way that it was just party intrigue. That it was a desperate plan by the opposition to stop the candidate's victory, which, according to them, was more than certain. Extremely angry to the point of making serious threats within four walls to those who tried to hinder their evil intentions. The millionaire was forced to appear in public, during a press conference, and gives voters her explanations:

— First of all, I would like to make it clear to all society in Pará that I am here just to respect each one of my voters. To clarify their doubts about the terrible accusations that the opposition is making on me, in a moment of complete despair to realize that our victory at the polls is certain. You use the name of my son, who died several years ago, to try to tarnish my reputation with each of you, made under great dedication to poorest communities in this state. I, however, publicly issue a challenge to my accusers: Let them prove their denunciations or get out of our way so that we can continue advancing towards victory.

The eloquent candidate was applauded by the whole crowd of listeners. With the exception of a few opponents, he was sure that he would once again have won the confidence of his voters. Meanwhile, elsewhere, the next step in the political attack on the businesswoman was carefully traced, making sure that Luís was already mentally capable of witnessing her in court. A hearing with both parties was scheduled and on the date chosen by the court.

Prosecution and defense appeared in court to clarify the allegations made against the millionaire. During the meeting open to the public, the defendant was interrogated by the State's defenders and she remained firm in saying that she was innocent in the face of all the accusations made by the journalist.

Naomi did not even imagine that the main idea of tarnishing her image before voters came from the magistrate who judged the case. So little that his son was really alive and present there, at that very moment, to unmask her because of her evil deeds against him and several other innocent people. After two hours sitting on the dock and in the heavy rain of questioning The accused appeared to have been well guided by her many lawyers.

His answers were perfect and he conveyed to those present at the meeting that his innocence would be guaranteed by the jury. Since she remains firm in the belief that she is being victimized by a plot to prevent her candidacy for the state government. Which was not entirely true. However, minutes before the jury withdraws for recess and then returns with the verdict, a new strategy is used by prosecuting attorneys. They announce to the Honorable Judge one more element that would prove to be the culprit for all the complaints presented in the ongoing process.

Renowned criminal lawyer Lucinda Brandão takes the floor. And he asks the magistrate for permission to introduce the jurors to a character who would be the key to resolving that impasse once and for all. Everyone remained silent while that man got up and took his place for questioning. Always accompanied by the defender, he began to speak under oath.

At first, he answered the first questions, such as informing his full name, his origin, age, etc. Then he told his listeners his whole sad story. From his sad childhood on the banks of the Guajara River, in the lower Amazon until his arrival in the capital, the time he lived in Ver-o-Peso.

The millionaire's adoption and mental crisis, ending with her terrible life experience in a psychiatric hospital. Where he was later expelled and forced to live for five long years in complete misery and in the open. When he presented himself as the heir of the Velasco who was presumed dead by the accused, a great turmoil began that needed to be circumvented by security.

The defender then initiates the interrogation to try to thoroughly reveal to the jurors the suffering experienced by her client:

— Mr. Luís Gustavo, how could you prove to the jury that you really are who you say you are? how could you prove to the jury that you really are who you say you are? Do you have an identity document or other concrete proof to confirm your statements?

— Yes, Your Honor. After being rescued from the streets with the help of a great friend, I was admitted to one of the best clinics in this country to treat my mental disability and, after a year and six months, fully recovered, I removed new documents that I clearly identified. as being the person I just wrote

— Okay, hand them over to the prosecutor. Now explain to this court how you ended up in a psychiatric hospital. And why not return to the home of the accused after being expelled from the place where he lived for fifteen years?

— Well, I would rather inform those present in this court that it was quite difficult for me to regain clarity and the smallest details of my past. However, although there are still many obscure points in my memory, I will be quoting what I am sure I know to be true

For almost an hour he recounted his trajectory from the day he lost consciousness until then, after finding a cure. With that testimony the jury went into recess and half an hour later they returned with the final decision. The defendant in the lawsuit was found guilty on all charges and prevented from pursuing her candidacy, running for political office. In addition to being obliged to return to the son all his rights guaranteed by law. As heir to the immense patrimony. He became the sole heir to the immense fortune of the traditional Guimarães Velasco family.

What should be done immediately. In addition, she was forced to pay a large fine to the State. This fine was for escaping from prison for false testimony. The problem was that the businesswoman had adopted another child after she abandoned Luís Gustavo and gave her the same inheritance rights. In view of this impasse, it was necessary to share the assets, where each would receive equal shares.

Luís would take possession of his assets immediately, however, Naomi's other daughter would have to wait for her death. The old beggar was cured of that damned mental illness and became aware of reality again. For the first time, Pará society could see justice being done against powerful people, giving deserved rights to those who really needed it.

However, he still needed to try Naomi for the crime committed against the doctor. The same one who initially denounced her for abandoning her son in a psychiatric hospital, without later providing him with the necessary assistance. The criminal at first lost to her opponents on the charge of abandoning a disabled person, but did not intend to be arrested for the murder committed. Thus, he intended to take immediate measures to prevent his opponents from proving his involvement in the crime.

Again he hired the services of the same group of mercenaries to carry out the possible threat. The plan was to eliminate the main responsible for the complaints against the businesswoman, in this case the journalist Marilda Campos. Naomi was warned by Matias, who commanded the mercenaries. About the risk of her being immediately the principal author of the journalist's crime.

Because, according to the prosecution's understanding. The sentence suffered by the accused would occur very close. Naomi's biggest flaw was exactly the pride. Of never wanting to take anyone's advice. And it would be exactly that mistake of yours that would lead to complete failure. Even though she was warned, she used stubbornness and ordered the order given to be carried out and again a crime should be committed. However, things do not always go as planned and the attack went wrong.

The journalist left unscathed and denounced the millionaire as the one who ordered the assassination attempt. What was accepted by judge Alessandra who determined the arrest of the accused. Until the investigations were completed. As he was extremely influential and powerful, his lawyers appealed the decision made by the magistrate before the supreme court in Brasilia, which was accepted with the release of a habeas corpus that allowed to answer the new charges in freedom.

With the new aggravation in the millionaire's complicated judicial history, public opinion about her innocence fell by almost one hundred percent. People began to doubt its integrity and turned entirely in favor of its opponents. Supporting journalist Marilda campos.

Human rights groups marched. They walked the streets of the capital demanding punishment for the accused and her arrest if the charges against her were proven. The mansion of the alleged mastermind of the attempted murder, located on Avenue Braz de Aguiar, was taken over by protesters. They demanded justice and not even Naomi's full power prevented the huge crowd from standing in front of her residence. They protested the decision taken by the judge in Brasilia to prioritize the alleged criminal.

Due to so many demonstrations, the State Bar Association became involved. They were in favor of the society that demanded greater commitment from the authorities to clarify such crimes.

The issue that was local came to be seen as a problem at the national level. Because it discredited justice as a whole and that should be resolved immediately, with all this pressure from society and the Bar Association, there was no alternative for the Supreme Court to revoke the first decision. And it determines that she be kept under house arrest again until everything is properly clarified.

This was another of the great victories for a society thirsty for justice, as it could not be otherwise, the political party that previously supported the candidate for the government of the State turned against her. A surprising strategy. They sought to win popular support, aiming to win more votes in future elections. Upon realizing that the mother was sinking and that soon all her guilt for the crimes would be revealed. Carla Velasco, the child adopted by Naomi as soon as she got rid of her crazed son. Now almost thirty years old.

He simply decided to disconnect from the alleged criminal to avoid any relationship with his mistakes. The architect who became the owner of the entire empire of the millionaire businesswoman filed for possession of her assets with her mother still alive, since she would no longer be in psychological conditions to manage her assets, due to age and all the current situation in which she was involved. The decision was accepted by the courts and put into effect as soon as possible. The lady of rubber, title inherited from her ancestors. Who became the pioneers in rubber production in the Amazon.

Now lost its empire to the one he chose as a substitute for his first son, Luís Gustavo. When he was struck by an unexpected madness. The injustice committed against that innocent man who needed his understanding immensely at the worst moment of his life.

Now I was being charged by God or fate. Carla, unlike Luís, was equally ruthless and willing to do anything to discard her mother and take over the empire of the Velasco. A new hearing was scheduled to hear the case and this time it took place behind closed doors. Only prosecution and defense lawyers were allowed. Together with the judge and his advisers. It lasted four hours and in the end, when everyone left the court. Vast numbers of reporters and onlookers surrounded the place.

They were trying to get clarification on the final decision of the trial. But nothing was passed on to the press about the verdict. Only later, when the defendant withdrew safely.

A public prosecutor gave a press conference, and clarified all doubts. Naomi Guimarães Velasco was found guilty of her crimes and should be sentenced to twenty-five years in prison. This in a closed system, without the right to bail or visits. But, due to her advanced age, the sentence should be applied as a house arrest. The defendant was to live in complete isolation until the end of his days.

Except for having the right to a professional to take care of your health and the other domestic employees of the house. He lost the freedom to participate in any event or social gathering. Receive friends or family at home, travel to any region, Brazilian state or abroad. Since then, the entire control of his old assets has become the sole responsibility of his daughter Carla Velasco.

Who chose to live in a penthouse located in the port de Souza Franco neighborhood, one of the most beautiful and expensive areas of the capital. Leaving the condemned to the mercy of loneliness and abandonment.

Just as she did to her son, when he became disabled. She kept in contact only with the employee responsible for the mansion to give orders. Also know the mother's current situation. That she was secluded in her room. Very rarely did he exchange a word or two with the elderly woman and almost always claiming to be in a hurry for the many commitments. Married to a senator from the republic, she lived most of the time in Brasilia, she did not sympathize with her mother's isolation. Nor did he care for his good.

She was ambitious to the extreme, driven by power and her life was filled with luxury and a good table. Completely opposed to Luís Gustavo, who despite being thrown out into the open still sought as much information as possible about the adoptive mother.

Several times he paid employees to let him know about his health. When stabilizing economically, he had as a first priority to return to Marajó to try to find his real parents and siblings, as well as the whole family.

In order to provide them with help, I brought the younger brothers to the big city. And it gave each of them the necessary condition so that they could live and raise their children in the capital, giving them a good education.

About his parents, he placed them in a large and luxurious apartment and until the end of their days they had no need. His good character distinguished him from Carla and made him much more worthy of divine blessings.

Informed about the decay of the former employer and that her entire fortune would now be with Carla, Martim and his cronies decided to take advantage of the situation. And they prepared your kidnapping. Without realizing it she continued in her normal routine until the first opportunity they kidnapped her. Now all attention is turned to Naomi's daughter taken by criminals.

Luís Gustavo, upon learning of the incident, immediately went to the police to request action on the case. Always with the support of Marilda and Judge Alessandra, the daring bandits kept her in captivity for about ten days. Always demanding from the husband and other family members the high amount of ten million reais, otherwise they would kill her.

The society followed on the news all the details of the negotiation and the local police did their best to try to locate them, but in vain. And, in the face of the strong threats made by criminals, the family relented. Planning to pay the required amount, even against the will of the investigators.

As a means of leveraging negotiations or finally arresting the hijackers. The feds were asked to get involved in the case. With advanced investigative techniques and greater experience in kidnappings, the agents took over the situation. And on the twelfth day of intense suspense about what the end of the plot involving the millionaire heiress of the Velasco would be like.

What seemed to have become routine for those people to experience intense problems. As there was a delay in the decision to pay the amount requested from the bandits, they started to act. More aggressively in order to show that they were not kidding. So they sent Paulo Ricardo, Carla's husband, a small box, packed as a gift.

The surprise when the package was opened was immense, because inside it was one of the woman's fingers. Exactly what she wore in her wedding ring, terror washed over everyone, who wept in desperation.

All demanded more effort from the authorities to rescue it from the power of criminals. Paulo knew the whole story of the relationship between Martim and his mother-in-law Naomi.

The contracts made by her in order for him and his cronies to carry out commissioned crimes and she immediately suspected that they were responsible for the abduction of his wife. He decided to reveal to the police everything he knew and left them aware of a small place located a few kilometers from the capital, where they used to meet to organize the plans of the former employer, before executing them. Both he and Carla knew about all Naomi's dirty acts, but kept a secret to avoid harming her. However, given the current situation, it was no longer possible to remain silent. So he had to tell everything about what he knew.

With the new information in hand, the police were efficient in their action. They immediately went out in search of capturing the criminals and trying to rescue the victim alive. Within hours the place where the kidnappers were supposed to be was surrounded. They did not expect this type of action from the police.

This is because it was agreed in advance that the husband would pay the ransom and Martim was already with two more cronies to get the money. While the rest of the group awaited the return of the crime partners.

He kept the hostage locked in a dark room and without any comfort. The feds surround and invade the house, covering them with gunfire, without giving them any chance of resistance. Even with that attitude, they almost put Carla's life at risk. But, despite the risk, the operation was a great success.

They immediately warned agents in the capital that the hostage was already free, so when Martim appeared at the ransom payment site he was arrested and arrested by federal agents.

The victim was released and handed over to family members who highly praised the efforts of the authorities involved in the case. With the gang broken up and his mentor arrested, everything is back to normal. All those moments of tension experienced by all led the two adoptive brothers to get closer and get to know each other better.

The arrogant millionaire has learned that no matter how great the power someone may have. Despite your material possessions or wealth, the worst can happen in your life at any time. For this reason, it is essential that you know how to value everything that is good, starting with the things considered the most common.

From a small friendship to a great love. The family, the true friends, the pet, the house where the home was built. All aspects of nature, a simple shower of rain on the roof.

Thus, his way of looking at life changed radically and the change could be seen in a short time. Instead of living as a socialite, snubbing power and greatness, she started to dedicate herself more to social services and to practice charity.

Together with her foster brother and Marilda, she took financial aid to beggars scattered throughout the city several times, then built a shelter for them, collecting them from the streets. Due to the various actions in favor of the poorest, voters came to want her or Luís to apply.

To be elected to public office in future elections and the proposal was accepted by Carla with affection. But he refused, as he had no political ambitions. Her goal was to reopen her old law school enrollment and complete her dream course.

He appealed to the court and received permission to enter the law course. Forming in this area. Four years after he was victorious in the fight against the one who once decided to throw him out into the open.

During his years in college he made great friendships with important people, however, he chose to give greater value to those closest to him. He started his relationship with the journalist Marilda Campos, with whom he later married. After graduating, he served as a public defender and passed a contest for prosecutors. Briefly exercising the new profession. Because he took another exam and held an important position as a judge in the Belem do Pará district.

During all these years of new achievements. Luís and his wife regularly visited the city squares and psychiatric hospitals, always helping as much as they could in the recovery and support of those who, like him, lost their reason. Most of the time collecting them under the shelter built on a large property acquired with the help of Carla Velasco. His most frequent spot was the Republic square, where he lived for so many years in complete abandonment. There, accompanied by his wife and two children. He remembered everything that happened and was grateful for the opportunity he received from God to meet Marilda.

Who helped him resume his lost life, conquer his dreams and the ideals of happiness. That Sunday he decided to play with his children. He had fun with Pedro Henrique and Carlos Eduardo on the green grass of the square, while his wife filmed the fun of the three to keep in the family's souvenir archive. Everything seemed to be perfect, the strength of love brought them together and promised to keep them happy forever. But fate had other plans for the couple.

And he wrote a different ending than they deserved. With the part of the inheritance received from Naomi. Luís bought fifty percent of Clarim's shares. And Marilda became a majority member of the most widely circulated newspaper in the state.

But she was passionate about journalism to the point that she didn't want to leave subordinates with important tasks. As she did the interviews and interesting articles, she was always in front of these services. In that period of new political campaigns she was invited by the republican party.

The same one where his sister-in-law Carla was competing to occupy the city hall to become head of the current mayor's office. Where he would have the chance to support her, doing what he loved most.

It turns out that, with just a month to go before voting starts, she had to take a last minute trip. He would go to the city of Manaus for an important conference on journalism, where people from all over the country would meet and it would be vitally important for his career. The flight was scheduled for that Friday at eight o'clock in the morning. Luís was terrified of flying and feared for his wife's safety, so he always chose the highest quality companies. Even if it was more expensive, because for him security came first.

However, not even the greatest care can change what destiny has designed. And, after a warm hug from her beloved husband and children, Marilda waves. He was there, without knowing it, his last goodbye. Then he settles on the commercial flight. It was heading towards the State of Amazonas.

It was customary for her to call home as soon as she reached her destination. He did this to warn that everything was fine. But on that particular day he did not receive a call from his wife, even though it was past the waiting time, worried he contacted the air flight agency to ask for an explanation of the plane's arrival at the destination and received repeated statements from that everything had gone smoothly, however, it didn't take long for the news to announce the accident.

They reported that there had been an air accident on a flight to Manaus that morning. Luís and the other family members hurried to confirm at the airport that the aircraft was the same as the one that took Marilda, and confirmation of the terrible tragedy came. It was not possible to describe the pain felt by Luís and all the family members at that moment, close friends mourned his loss. Carla mourned the death of her sister-in-law and friend intensely.

Alessandra, acting as a judge, ordered the Court's officials to mourn three days. And the governor of the state mourned the civil service for forty-eight hours. The two children of the couple remained from that beautiful union, they were Luís Gustavo's treasure and he has dedicated himself ever since to the gift that the deceased wife left him. That same year, six months after the tragedy that occurred in his life, Naomi also recluses in her house at the age of seventy-five. After graduating in law and occupying the important position of judge, Luís appeals to the Supreme Court in Federal City.

And it manages to ease the condemnation of the adoptive mother. He was allowed to receive visitors and leave the mansion on a walk at least twice a month. Despite these perks, she refused to make use of them and remained in the mansion.

His departure, regardless of all the evil done, left him with sadness in his heart. His routine became work, living with his children and wandering in complete solitude through the Republic square to remember the many times he was there with his wife, after returning from the madness that almost destroyed him. He walked everywhere, observing every detail of the place, reliving the five years he wandered around with that filthy bag over his shoulders.

The exact moment when Marilda came to do an interview that would lead him to have the chance to be cured. He would recover completely from the evil that enslaved him in the darkness. Losing the great love of her life was a tremendous emotional shock.

However, there was no risk of going crazy again because the treatment he did strengthened his brain tremendously. If it weren't for that, it would be the end of you. However, an immense pain was stuck in his chest, it would be difficult to definitively overcome the wound that burned inside him.

Consequently, I would never be able to love again. For in his view, no woman possessed the attributes of the one who once conquered him in an inexplicable way. Solitude was once again part of his existence. Even with the two children at his side, he couldn't stop thinking about his dead wife, every second he was awake. And even when I slept I had dreams.

Where he relived the good times they lived together. There was no point in encouraging family and friends to go out and have fun. In the hope that she would meet someone and fall in love again.

The mother and father were concerned about the sadness that ate at their son's soul. And they prayed a lot for him, for a miracle to happen and he would be happy again. But, apparently, the doors of his heart were closed to love.

His eyes could only see the image of the one he still loved. The world around him was limited to the time he met Marilda, the future seemed to him to be of no importance. All this bitterness of spirit, however, did not prevent him from remaining acting as an excellent judge, judging each case with clarity.

In fact, it was during his time at work that he had the most inner peace, but when he returned home at the end of the day, after giving all his attention to his two teenage children, what he was left with was loneliness in a room that even though it was well lit seemed completely darkness.

Lying on the soft bed, where for several years he slept beside his beloved woman, he gradually died of so much longing. Everything there brought back memories of her and the moments of intense pleasure they lived together, with her eyes closed she went back in time in a brief thought.

And he was able to daydream about the happiness and love that united them. It seemed that his world was over at the very moment he confirmed his wife's death. The ground beneath his feet opened and he would have been swallowed by the darkness that caused the pain and suffering that tore his heart. A curse or karma led him to the same end, alone and with no one to love him.

Living with family and friends does little to fill the void that has come to exist in your troubled soul. Like a man tired of suffering so many disappointments. I finally wanted to find peace and quiet, to love and be loved, to be able to come home and throw myself into the arms of his beloved and be someone fully realized. But the damn fate, which hated him, wrote a terrible ending for both of them. For Marilda, a sudden death, for him, the condemnation of a continuous search. For the chance to be happy, to start over.

Gradually it was completely isolated from reality, it was not crazy. just a strong need for privacy. He wanted space, to avoid disturbing him. At least, that's what he used to say to himself. In this idea of keeping his distance from those around him, he ended up being so absent from work that they decided to remove him.

He received permanent dismissal from his duties on the grounds that he would need to recover from the severe trauma he suffered from the tragedy that resulted in his wife's death. For him, who already longed for isolation, it was the best thing that could happen to him. Now he could definitely close himself in the shell and never have to leave.

Maternal grandparents took custody of their grandchildren. They claimed that their father did not have the minimum conditions to continue taking care of them. And that was a fact. Alone in the huge mansion, surrounded by the green of the many trees planted around it, a flower garden, where were the red roses and lilies that Marilda loved so much. For the depressive owner of that immensity of home, nothing existed. For him, the only place left was that from which he could watch the rain fall hidden behind the glass with dark films without anyone seeing it. Outside, the usual rain falls gently.

Madness - Fiction Romance

Dripping its drops of water through the fogged glass that is prevented from reaching its viewer. Everything seemed stopped, especially time. Only the wind blew calmly from the four corners of the farm, parading through the balcony of the spacious house painted in white and blue.

Birds were no longer heard because they retired. They were all saddened to their nests, trying to escape the cold and protect their young from the danger of the night that would soon come.

The lonely man remained reclining. Behind the wide window watching the void before your eyes for hours, but it wasn't really there. It flew in his thoughts, in the memories where he stuck since he lost his great love. As the living dead simply vegetated, he saw no reason to move on.

So little to believe that something good could happen to the point of helping him to overcome all that pain that burned in his chest. Another day is over and what he has left is to realize that he remains within four walls. Isolated from everything and everyone like a frightened animal, I wake up by the immense loneliness that insists on accompanying him.

Insomnia prevented him from sleeping, his eyelids darkened by dawns without rest, showing tremendous physical wear. Due to the distressing situation in which he found himself. Without eating properly for days at a time you will slowly languish.

And nothing and nobody would change that, because it was his decision. Your choice to punish yourself for considering yourself unfortunate. With no luck, a poor devil undeserved to have a happy ending.

He had been locked in that mansion for weeks, without giving any news to friends and family, nor answering the phone, no one knew for sure how he could be. He had dismissed all employees, opted for the right not to be disturbed. The property that used to be quite popular has become deserted, the grown grass has started to fill with weeds.

That spread quickly across the land. The lights were turned off and there was only darkness in their place. Everything was darkness at sunset. Concerned, some of his closest friends and brothers went to see him, but to no avail.

The gates will remain closed, inaccessible, nor will the dogs bark announcing the arrival of visitors. Because they were no longer there, they were sent away with those who treated them. Alone, without any other company, that was his option.

The poor boy who lived all his childhood as a riverside, bathing on the banks of the Guajará River, in the lower Amazon, who before beginning had a dream. That even in his adolescence he courageously ran away to try his luck in the big city.

Who was graced by becoming the heir to one of the most traditional families in the region. He who, by a damned plot of fate, ended up with a terrible madness that undid his plans to reach the summit of his dreams and threw him down the bank, turning him into a filthy rag.

The same fate that put an angel in his path and helped him to rise again. That restored everything he had lost during the twenty years of obscurity, yes. He himself brought him back to reason and allowed him to be happy.

Now again took everything from him and threw him into a drug that was almost unbearable. How to survive so much hardship? Would he still have strength left? Were they enough to go beyond where you managed to get with so much difficulty?

Only time would be able to answer such questions. He himself had no way of knowing, because he lost the will to fight. Death reached and killed the soul that moved within its inert body.

Paralyzed by the sadness that filled him with torment and pain. While Luís Gustavo savored the bitter taste of defeat again. Their children lived fully in wealthy childhood.

Surrounded by pampering by the grandparents who tried hard to erase from their memories the father they always saw as a lunatic. For in-laws, despite everything he achieved after healing. Even his high position as a renowned judge of law, they could not see him or accept him as worthy of being part of the family.

They hated to know that their daughter, in whom they wished to achieve great fulfillment, chose to marry a homeless person. Dropped by the banks and gazebos of the squares in the company of others without roofs. Their efforts to erase the shameful past that they had, the many years they lived as a wretch, wandering the streets in a deplorable state did not matter. Nothing would erase the stain of poverty that he brought with him, he would always be seen for what his roots meant and not for what he built in the course of his life. This mediocre prejudice of those who find themselves in the highest social standards is what often prevents someone from climbing the pyramid and equaling them.

In the opinion of these callousers, each one is born in the right class. Some on top, others in the middle and the base formed by those that God has reserved to serve as a platform at your feet. Did God really have such a vision to deal with his creatures? Would he make such a sense of people to the point of separating a miserable people to serve exclusively other superiors?

If that is possible, then why did you choose to send your Son into this world as a carpenter. Since he is the owner of the entire universe? Was he falling into contradiction and claiming it was an honor to be born poor? Who knows! The truth was that the arrogant did not bother to accept him as the one who deserved the rightful place.

And they taught its fruits to see it as a tree unworthy to remain planted in the same land as them. Some months passed and during all that time he had no contact with the two teenagers.

He lived in prison in that house, trapped by memories. Marilda, before her departure to the afterlife, left a work written in two volumes completed, which told the story of overcoming lived by the husband. After reading and rereading the text several times, he decided to send it to an editor for publication. He left the cocoon after so much absence, but only for a short time.

The book, entitled " Deserted streets", was very well accepted by readers and did not take long to become a best seller. This aroused in him the desire to publish other works, transforming his solitude into art. He missed his kids, but he didn't have to worry, they were in great hands. He was present in most of his childhoods, he was a present, loving father, a good listener, he had done his part well.

Even more than a day he received from his parents. Now they would go on without their father's shadow and learn to survive alone, as he himself learned to do. On rare occasions, they saw him appear in front of the property, collecting mail or answering deliveries.

Most of the time he remained distant from the view of the curious. It was rarely possible to see him near the window on the side of the property, some paparazzi surround the property in search of news to print on the front page of gossip magazines and newspapers, but for him all that advertising harassment did not bother him. In his view, they didn't even exist, they didn't add up. He switched the hours looking at the exterior of the house, through smoked glass, through the colored screen of a computer.

Where he transformed his creative thoughts into literary texts, after the publication of " deserted streets" he wrote several new works. Staying in that huge house was a choice he made to always be close to the memories of his deceased wife, but at that time of the championship it no longer made any sense, it was time to leave the past and walk towards the future. However, he continued with the intention of keeping himself away from people and reality that might want to make him look back.

The End

As he owned several properties, he handed over the mansion to the care of his two younger brothers and moved to a penthouse located in the well-known Manoel Pinto da Silva building, the largest and tallest building in the capital of Pará at that time, with luxurious apartments, built still in the seventies in front of also no less known and frequented square of the republic.

From the top of the more than forty floors, it was possible to see the admirable panorama of the city of mango trees. As Belém was popularly known. And admire all the green divided between diverse types of vegetation. His gaze hovered over everything the vision could achieve.

The center of the square, the bandstands where he slept for so many years lying on the filthy floor. The historical monuments, the small improvised lake where the birds drank or wet their down. Couples holding each other or walking hand in hand along the narrow walkways.

So many years went by and those images didn't seem to want to leave his mind tired of coming and going. Ups and downs, but performed in the face of countless experiences.

He slept late and woke up very early to start writing his poems or another chapter in a novel. In a few years he became one of the most popular writers in the North of Brazil. And its greatest feature was the fact that it was able to publish up to six new works during a year, something unprecedented in Brazilian literature.

Writers generally take about six months to a year to publish a book, while it presents its readers with triple that amount.

Luís Gustavo's loneliness and frequent losses made him an unusual literary, capable of creating stories full of realism and romanticism like never before read. His works soon sold out on bookstore shelves and the local media began to comment on the importance of his work. Taking criticism to praise his prestige as the greatest poet and novelist of Pará in recent decades, with this huge achievement and the value as an illustrious person in society, his in-laws who rejected him.

Due to their dark past, they had to recognize his value and started to support him, despite the fact that he did not care about it, and endeavored to fix all the negative information they had implanted about their father in the minds of their grandchildren. It didn't matter to Luís whether he was loved by his children or not, that would seem insensitive on his part.

But he learned to be unique in the world. He didn't miss anyone's attention, except for the woman who once held out his hands. Taking him out of the pit. The routine was the same, creating and publishing new works and receiving the affection, respect and recognition deserved from the public.

But that night his worst enemy, fate, had a surprise in store for him. The publisher decided to make a cocktail to launch the fortieth title of the author, three times best seller of the year and the chosen environment was the municipal library.

The place was full of fans that weekend was the biggest attraction of the last days. Among so many distinguished people, one in particular caught his attention. That beautiful woman with red hair was exaggeratedly like Marilda. Both in its physical aspect and in the delicate way of expressing and smiling. He approaches in awe, his eyes shining at the same moment they were enchanted by such similarity.

She turned to receive him, after all, he was the host of the ceremony. There were eight who exchanged opinions about the event, all of them received it with a wide smile. Because he just signed dozens of books sold and decided to get up to walk around and greet his guests. She extends a delicate hand to him to kiss her, as was the custom of that time, and identifies himself:

— Nice to meet you, Eduarda Lira

— Charmed

— The event is beautiful, I always wanted to meet you in person.

But my many commitments prevented me. Today, however, I was able to attend the launch of yet another of his works

— I don't remember seeing her signing any book

— Yes, it is true.

My daughter was the person who had the honor of going to you to get the autograph

— I understand. Married, I suppose

— No, widow just over a year ago

— But already, so young?

— True, unfortunately death is sneaky.

You don't choose color or age. arrives suddenly and takes without notice

— Yes, I agree

— As far as I know about you, he also lost his wife during a plane crash

— Yeah, as you just said, life comes to an end when you least expect it

The conversation lasted for a few hours, starting in the meeting wing and extending to the building's courtyard, from where they proceeded to the garden that separated the place from the street in which several vehicles passed. Approaching twenty-two o'clock, the guests were saying goodbye to the writer, praising the event and the published work. Eduarda and her teenage daughter thank the attention and leave. Not before he received from his admirer a small card with the telephone number and the request for him to call later. And that is what he actually did as soon as he got to the penthouse, where he lived.

He conversation then continued until the early hours of the morning. They made an appointment for the next day, first went to dinner at one of the many restaurants in town and then Luís invites her to visit his apartment.

What she dares not refuse. After three or four glasses of a French drink and confessions full of burning desire, the first kiss rolled. That event was unique to both of them after they lost the great love of their lives.

Since Marilda left Luís Gustavo, she lived in total isolation, without pleasure and sex. The same would have happened with the new partner, a widow not long ago. It even looked like a plot of fate, because their paths crossed bringing similar stories into the sketch.

Both lost the people they loved and had decided not to give in to other passions. He plunged headlong into literature and she into work to try to fill the immense void that remained inside her chest.

Even her professions were the same, Eduarda, too, was a lawyer and had the intention of becoming a law judge soon. Luana, the teenage daughter, loved meeting her mother's new boyfriend, mainly because he is a writer and she dreams of following her example.

Nothing could be more perfect, I was even afraid that all that perfection would come to an end. But that was not going to happen, God or mischievous fate decided to stop playing tricks on him and finally let him be happy.

The couple's marriage bond took place on Christmas Eve that same year. The highly refined party took place in the main hall of the Paraense Assembly, the hottest festive area in the capital. Place where only the highest society used to gather for very important events. At the same time, another of his long-awaited works is published, the title conveyed to readers the idea of completing a long journey.

"Finally Love" was the story of the two lovers who found in each other the longed-for happiness. It was the end of the relentless search for peace that everyone longs to find

End